May, 1924

Against the teal, the canvas-veil, the sunlight's lemon pen arrived. Superlunary approval- it spilt its ink against the sky. Agreeing breeze, the ozone's bliss- the document the sun had signatured. Witnessed by lakes of dewey grass, the sunlight wrote tomorrow's wedding speech; the sunlight's cursive wedding speech. A paling blue, from ill Neptunes, inside the endless courtroom of Heaven's sea, against the skin of teal balloons, the sunlight wrote tomorrow's wedding speech; the sunlight's cursive wedding speech.

The beetle blurb, a black color; the automobile's black bonnet. Mechanically burping purred from that galloping black comet. Below ivory colored fluff, the automobile quickened past the grass. Against the endless rug of lime the whizzing wheels released dust's careless ghost. Their wheels released dust's careless ghost. The clouds of pearl, their whipping whirls, watched the black automobile leak by meadows, reflecting on the black roof's curl. Those whizzing wheels released dust's careless ghost. Their wheels released dust's careless ghost.

A kiwi scent, excited sweat- perspiration's syrup perfume paranormally spread its scent amongst three young adults amused. The driver male, passenger girl, as the driver's sister laughed behind them. Three inside the bullet on wheels. Three young adults who laughed against the wind. Three young adults against the wind. A raven speed, between the green, as if that emerald Heaven ate a sin. And laughter crooned, the careless suite of young adults who drove against the wind. Three young adults against the wind.

Sobek was the one driving with his fiancee seated in the passenger seat next to him. Lennena Bloo, her smile almost became as hauntingly pearly hued as her skin, which turned to ivory when in any light. All of her, even the yellow sundresses she favored, became a new shade of lemon all below her blonde hair, bowing into unclaimed colors like worshippers.

In the back seat was Sobek's three year younger sister, Sadie, who had a similar resemblance to her brother.

Sobek...

His hair was that verdant color of black. So wetly black, it tried becoming spruce, with glaring gel almost about to hatch, and leak throughout the strands all bouncing loose. The buttoned shirt almost appeared too clean beneath the cracking in his ratty grin which summoned dirt away from fearful scenes, and told the world he'd witnessed everything. He rarely missed a scale of confidence as his boyish manner kept him humble, and wrapped up his movie-style appearance; a mafia croc, avoiding trouble. But Lennena Bloo treasured her Sobek, and Love became the bow atop his head.

And Sobek realized who he was when Lennena Bloo called him hers. She'd ruffle his hair. She made him smile just enough. She kept him as him.

Lennena Bloo started buttoning up his shirts. And like a harp rebelling, calmer notes began from out his mouth. His smile escaped its guilt-conviction when above her gentle touch. Every rising finger said they'd pull away any wrinkles. Lennena Bloo loved to button up Sobek's shirts. The scales of one another's smile began to button when they'd kiss after.

And then Lennena Bloo...

Lennena never liked the flapper life. Her lemon hair hated gel anyway, for it avoided lampposts during night as lemon hair stayed in museums' hallways. She was creeping on the floor of learning as her former peers experimented. And as hangovers haunted their mornings, she steered through forest after forest den. The deer explored her footprints left behind after strolls of reading through the forest, sniffing novel shadows from Oscar Wilde while Lennena Bloo returned home to rest. After that, she'd kiss her Sobek goodbye before she saw her museum 9 to 5.

Behind the couple, Sadie, like a guardian angel...

And a little sister's voice was curing whenever the siblings mourned their brother, who died from Spanish Flu one hot morning. Half-cracked sibling smiles, mourning together. But a healing suite began with coffee when the siblings went to Salem cafes. In the Salem streets they laughed at worry as jokes and sarcasm kept it away. Two years younger, the sibling brothers need, she kneaded everyday with the dough of joking's steam, and just overall being sweet and good at heart.

"These fields are gorgeous." Lennena noted in a tone almost able to seduce the sun into turning that valley of lime colored grass into actual emeralds. She turned to her fiance, asking. "Why are you speeding past them?"

Sobek had no good answer, maintaining the racing speed down the strip of tan and dirt road. He stammered with a voice worried about not matching the speed of the automobile. "We'll take a slower cruise on the way home. Show you the fields, Lennena."

Lennena turned around to face Sadie in the back, and asked. "Have you seen these fields, Sadie?"

"Yes." Sadie said. "I'd say, we'll catch the plains on a sunny day like this wicked rarely."

"Goodness," Lennena sighed, "they should always remain this way."

She looked out the passenger window, and turned her sigh into a sort of thankful longing. "It's like a spinning lake of emeralds, Sobek."

Sadie chimed in. "It is- austerely beautiful. I swear, Lennena, when Sobek and- and I were kids, we never saw the fields this way."

"The fields know it's our wedding day tomorrow." Sobek said in an almost sort of humming voice. He sounded honest, but his remark was as good a shout for help in a caving-in mine until his fiancee responded. His fiancee always responded. But he always felt to be in a cave when they were on about their days and apart, so he stayed silent then.

"Oh," Lennena said with a thankful twinkle on her smile, "they do. And they want to congratulate us, Sobek. Let's slow down and listen."

Sadie chimed. "I'm getting tired of the grumbling engine anyways. Listen to your woman, Sobek."

"I do." Sobek shrugged with a nonchalant tone, keeping that motorcar galloping at a fiery pace.

Listen to your woman. Sobek and Lennena could have smiled at this after taking no time to almost telepathically recall how they cuddled up and read together.

They rarely read separate books. When Sobek stumbled across Lennena Bloo in the foliage forest that autumn day back in 1922, in a warm and shy afternoon in November, she was skimming the lines of a copy of Shakespare's *Midsummer Night's Dream*. Confused, he asked her the obvious question, and she explained how she just enjoyed reading the soliloquies. Of course, the conversation continued with him asking what in the bloody hell a soliloquy was. He learned about the iambic meter that day, and they've been swooning over it ever since. He loved hearing her speak iambically. She loved how he looked when he listened to her. Last night she got to see that doughy expression of satisfied wonder, and he got to listen to her.

"I listen." He moped, burying a smirk that allowed his grip to tighten on the steering wheel.

Lennena made a poor attempt at rolling her eyes in a teasing manner to retaliate her fiance's confidence, for she rarely even remembered it was something people did. "He does."

She fixed herself, bouncing in the passenger seat instead of trying to roll her eyes. "You do- every now and then."

The fields were nice, but Lennena's smile was nicer, and wasn't flying past the motorcar's windows. No matter how fast he was going, she was right there. In the race of life, he found his angel. As Lennena looked at him, she wasn't sure what he was, but she sure knew she'd be a fool to let him go. Whenever she looked at him, she heard the subtle and muffled static gramophone of her memory gurgle like a dove learning to coo. It was in that almost cracking voice of his. *What's a soliloquy?* Thence, her eyes always, *always,* hushed *I'll tell you* whenever she looked at him.

Lennena took another strain of seconds watching that affable shade of green escape away. She turned to her fiance again, begging. "Oh, can't you slow down?"

Her begging tone made him regret his speed.

"I-I'm just excited to get everything in order." Sobek said, keeping the speed.

"Darling, it will be." Lennena assured. "Can't we stop rushing past this place of your childhood?"

"On our way home. I promise." Sobek said with a nod. "This is why I took the backroads, guys. I like this secluded way, you know?"

Sadie snickered. "Where's his lying face?"

Lennena looked at her man's face. Sobek was a horrific liar on account of nervously smiling every time he told a lie. It was a smile too shy to be a smile.

"He's being honest, Sadie." Lennena said, keeping her gaze upon the lines upon her fiance's lips.

"I like driving through this way because no one else knows about it." Sobek confessed, sounding tired.

"Wait." Sadie croaked, leaning towards the front so her noggin may enter between Lennena and Sobek. "And where will you be while we pick up the dresses?"

Sobek cracked the teasing smirk. "Not getting whiskey."

"Quit your messing," Lennena said with a sharp look in her eyes, "or else I may not kiss you at the altar tomorrow."

"No. You'll kiss me."

"And he's gonna cry." Sadie teased.

"Are you gonna cry?" Lennena asked in the same tone that she had when marvelling at the grass flying past the automobile. And she began to smile when she watched how that man began to try and hide his nervous smile while he ribbitted.

"Wha-ha? No." He slapped the steering wheel, almost chuckling. "I'm not gonna cry."

"Oh! He's gonna cry!" Sadie cheered.

The automobile slowed ever so slightly to a barely noticeable extent as something heavier began stepping on the gas in his mind, making his foot on the gas lighter. Lennena watched her man think.

She reached over and laid her palm upon his leg, hushing. "I'll be right with you. Honey, it'll be alright. Right in front of you."

"I know." Sobek exhaled, relieved.

"Oh my goodness." Sadie slouched back in the back seat again. "He *is* going to cry."

"Yeah." Sobek sighed. "What are you gonna do if I cry?"

"Love you all the same." Lennena said assuredly. "The Earth rains every now and then."

"Something to keep those fields watered, fresh and like they are now, huh." Sobek said. He sounded excited like someone in a classroom on their own accord. This excitement was only because of Lennena Bloo though.

"I promise, guys." Sobek said with an oddly choreographed nod. "I'll stop the car by this road on our way home."

The drive continued into Salem as the town appeared asleep. Lampposts kept their eyes closed, only giving the turquoise melodies of May their pale-glass eyelids.

Even in May, Salem still adored October. An autumn crispness haunted every building with cruci-kisses, like texts banished from libraries due to erotic passages. Every red apartment building sang a song about the Fall.

Even in May, Salem still adored October, the way a soul will stumble after healing after a toxic lover.

"Why are we taking the long way?" Sadie asked.

It was true. Sobek was taking the long way, driving down seemingly meaningless rows of apartments. Barely anyone inhabited the sidewalks in some of the roads he sent the motorcar down.

Sobek shrugged. "I, uh-"

"It's alright." Lennena chirped, watching the dirtily tan bracks and curtained windows wave hello and goodbye to them. "I like this way. All this dirty old brick'll make the fields friendly, even if the sun isn't there when we're going back."

"It'll be there." Sobek promised again, making strange notice of the signs on the corners of the street. He was particularly keeping an eye out for signs that would lead him down a certain road in Salem. He wanted to keeps his eyes from one particular church in the town.

"The girls should have had their cab drop them off at the house by now." Lennena guessed in a voice that almost retold an unhappened memory, like a gardener predicting which plant would grow first. She had immense hope in her predictions. "Probably talking to your grandmother currently."

There was a thoughtful pause, or a pretendingly thoughtful one at least.

"I wonder what stories they'd be telling her." Lennena continued, wanting to fill the void of talking in the car.

Sobek shrugged, halfly smiling at some room of memories in his mind. "All of them."

The smile said it all. He'd really like to know what they were talking about back at the estate. He always enjoyed listening to her.

Sobek parked the automobile in a spacious and unfull parking lot outside of a marble-white building in an obscure part of Salem after driving through the town for a good three minutes or so.

The first floor had pillars between its obtuse windows, but creamy curtains hid what was truly inside the building. And, before the three disembarked from the automobile, those creamy curtains warned about tomorrow while the sun was forcing kiss after kiss against their ruffles, trying to keep everyone that was the curtains silent.

The three entered into an illuminously white lobby full of white sofas, manikins in wedding dresses, an abandoned desk, a yellow rug, one wall with an army rank of mirrors, and a whole lot of space in the middle of everything, just hovering imprisoned all above the yellow rug.

With the two women of the trio being brisk, Sobek walked with the littlest limps. It was barely noticeable, but it was there, and it was his only tattoo from his one month stay aboard a prison ship back in 1919 when he was 18.

While Sadie and Lennena talked with an employee, a cheery chickadee-like woman, Sobek stood before the manless sofa. He had his hands in his black pants' pockets rather awkwardly as the three women talked. He was too *something* to sit or talk, and he would not let anyone know what somethings were, unless it was with Lennena Bloo in private.

After a three minute conversation, Sadie went into a changing room, and returned back into the lobby in a yellow bridesmaid dress.

"Oh, Sadie." Lennena chirped. "You're magnificent."

"Won't all the girls look absolutely stunning in these?" Sadie clucked to her future sister-in-law.

As Sobek's eyes remained a little disinterested, Lennena's lit up. She agreed. "Sisters in yellow. Truly-you're truly brilliant picking yellow, Sadie."

"You know why she picked it, right?" Sobek gruffed, feeling comfortable that the employee was off in another room.

"Yellow?" Lennena chirped, to which Sadie began in a teasing tone of memory. "Lellow. He used to say lellow."

Lennena's lips lept into a smile as if they had just exited a lake of frowns; drying in amusement. "Lellow!"

"And now," Sobek said with a halfly-cracked smile as he too examined the dress his sister wore, "we got lellyellow dresses for the bridesmaids for our wedding. Yellow ties for the groomsmen. Yellow ties choking all of them."

"And what's choking you tomorrow?" Lennena asked with a smirk that belonged somewhere else as she aimed it at her man.

He answered, smirking back in a more teasing manner. "The pink tie you picked for me."

"It'll make your blushing face less noticeable." Lennena declared in a teachery tone. "Sobek, you'll look adorable."

Sobek looked at her. The ultimate belief was glossing that somewhat silent gaze, and that became a calm appearance about his eyes whenever they looked at each other.

"The dresses match your hair, Lennena." Sobek chimed. Lennena kept their gazes locked, so did Sobek, as she teased. "My hair, the lellow dresses, you-"

"Awwwww." Sadie said, dropping her shoulders in an upside-down shrug of bliss. She glued her squinting gaze against her brother and future sister-in-law, basking in the sight of the two standing in front of the creamy curtains. She sighed. "If that's the way you two will be standing before the altar tomorrow then Imma cry too."

"No one's crying tomorrow." Sobek laughed, forgetting how that one smile cracked against his lips. Lennena aimed that adoring look at the smile of fibs, and she smiled at it. He looked at her. Instantly, his smile morphed into an honest one like hers, and he became silent in honesty, no longer having to laugh a lie about not crying tomorrow. She fixed his smile as simply as the way she buttoned up his shirts.

"Marry me." Sobek said as he popped his eyebrows up.

"I will." Lennena smiled.

"Oh!" The employee cheered upon stumbling out from another room, carrying bags of the dresses. She complimented Sadie. "That is a gorgeous dress. Oh! Just beautiful."

"Thank you." Lennena said, speaking in the cheerful voice she often used in the museum when schools would bring kids over for some of the exhibits. "It's the bridesmaids' dresses for tomorrow."

The employee's face lit up. Her eyes read and reread the sight of Sobek and Lennena. She smiled. "And it's you two?"

"Yes." Lennena said with a tilting head that pulled at the smile on her fiance's face.

"Awww." The employee gasped. "You're so pretty together."

Lennena spoke for her and her fiance. "Thank you."

"Ah." Sadie said. "They certainly are. I don't know about the groom- but his bride sure is a catch, huh? Imma go slip out of this so it's not wrinkled for tomorrow, Lennena."

"Alright, Sadie." Lennena responded with a smile.

With Sadie getting changed in a dressing room, Lennena and the employee chatted as Sobek zoned out in the overly white room.

It was as if the valley had waited for them. Everything was even more diamondly than before, shimmering the lime color of green. Every tiny blade of Massachusetts' timid grass absorbed the dew from hours and hours ago, and now it all had that natural lotion embedded in its land. Thus, the twinkle.

"I told you." Sobek said with a pleased smile as he exited the automobile. He had parked it on the side of the lonely tan road.

The symphony of opening and closing automobile doors humphed, sending black echoes into that available distance, that available green-diamond distance.

"Sobek." Lennena whined with a thankful pout as she stomped towards her Sobek. She crumbled against his chest, hugging him as she moped. "It's so pretty."

"Yeah." Sobek agreed. He wrapped his arms around her, and gently rubbed her back while peering out at the vastness. "Lennena."

"Yes?"

"Let's take some photographs in this very field after the wedding is said and done tomorrow."

Lennena opened her eyes to smile against Sobek's chest. The buttons of his white shirt dug into her cheek like scales. She inhaled and deeply let the sigh escape against his chest before she spoke again. "Use that mind for good, Sobek."

Sobek laughed a shy and single *aha*.

Sadie entered the scene, and stood a bit away from the couple. For a moment, a moment as silent as a cloud, the three just looked out against the seemingly endless plain of twinkling glass below an austerely lightly shaded sky like forgiven misers looking at their riches.

"If only we brought a camera or something." Sobek said. "We could've captured this moment right in the grass, the grass we love so well, and show our future children a photo of their mom and dad... just before they got married."

Lennena chimed in. "Then we'll bring them here one day. Let them loose here."

She watched him smile.

"Sobek." Lennena whined. She dug her chin deeper against him. "We'll get the pictures tomorrow."

"I wanna be the one to take it." Sadie declared. "I'm good at taking pictures."

"Good at making me look goofy in them." Sobek chirped. Sadie shook her head, and retorted. "This is a serious matter, brother. Besides, imagine it, something like that framed in a living room... ah-above a fireplace, in a den, in a bedroom. In your bedroom."

Lennena and Sobek looked at the youngest of the trio. It was said in their eyes. Somehow, Sadie's little vocal ramble made tomorrow closer. That emerald apparel over that addicting lime color of grass was tar against her lingering speech, and everything combined then to truly tell the breeze above the grass that every gust was welcome to the wedding.

"I'm telling you, Sadie," Sobek exclaimed, pointing his finger at his little sister, "go to school for photography."

Sadie and Lennena shared smiles of disbelief. Sobek was too good at hyping up others. He seemed to take some strange enjoyment out of it- watching others catch their butterflies of hope in their bare hands.

Sobek slipped his hand back in his pocket while his other arm remained around Lennena. He turned his tone into a disappointed bout of relief, soft, like water apologizing to sand. "That's why I'm glad you aren't turning out like one of those flapper girls. You got plenty of good things going for you, Sadie."

"She does." Lennena shrugged her head, wondering if she should agree with her fiance. "Y-you do." She said to Sadie in a clearer tone.

"I don't know why you don't like flappers." Sadie gruffed. She disliked when their dad judged people as well, and it was strange when her older brother did so too.

He had no good reply that he felt comfortable enough to say. After a bit of pondering, he dug his hand deeper into his pocket, squeezed Lennena tighter against him, and exhaled. "They're deceiving photos underneath all that pale and art deco gold they wear."

"Not all of them." Sadie said defensively.

Discomfort draped Lennena's face while examining the competing expressions of the siblings. They both seemed to force an expression of fake disinterest. She was too scared to agree vocally with Sobek, but a part of her *did* agree with him, while feeling no use in judging anyone.

"But will the sun still be out by the time everything about the wedding and wedding dinner is done?" Lennena asked, bringing the attention of the three back to the fields.

Sobek sighed an okay sigh with a reassuring tone to his voice. "Then the next morning, darling, before we leave for our honeymoon."

Something chugged against the earth. The trio perked up, and squinted out upon the distance to see a train beginning its crossing over the horizon of twinkling lime.

Lennena and Sadie saw just a train, but Sobek looked like he had just been shot. Neither his bride nor sister noticed as they watched the long bodied train pass across the valley in the distance.

"I bet it's going to Back Bay Station." Lennena suggested. She buried her chin even deeper against Sobek's chest, mumbling. "We should take a train to travel somewhere, Sobek."

The groom almost became a ghost aboard the train. If passengers saw phantoms, they'd see his crocodile eyeballs. Burning letters wrote themselves again as that escaping train crawled. A smog polluted bliss's lime color when trains galloped by. The groom almost became a ghost aboard the train. His crocodile eyeballs watched its chugging kill the merry month of May.

"You alright, Sobek?"

Sobek looked down at Lennena. Her sweet chime had broke him out of a trance as the train vanished out of sight. Its chugging lingered like a ghost as the bride and groom looked into each others' eyes.

"I'm alright." He moped.

Ashy residue befell upon the valley. Like a warning black as coal, evaporated by the sunlight, the train hiccuped its clouds of smog above the grasses' diamond shine. And like the broken veil of widows, that nebulous snowfall's ashy residue befell upon the valley; just a sprinkle shade of grey proposing on the twinkling grass softly.

The scent of steam and melting steel phantomly lingered to the three upon the road in the plain of grass. The grass was silent again as if trains were not even invited yet. Something primal, and quiet, haunted them then as they looked at tomorrow on the grass, on their lime colored future.

"You look like you just saw a ghost, baby." Lennena teased. No longer did any echoes stain the spring-time air, but a smog remained in Sobek's eyes as he confessed. "No. I saw a train."

Night arrived in a withering gown of orange outside the estate of Sobek and Sadie's parents. Sobek bought the three story mansion for his parents a few months back on account of his good luck in the "bond business". The crimson painted exterior of the estate was rather inviting to the blossoming spirit of the night, taking hospitality on her while seeing how her orange garments withered into darker shades.

A sort of last-call bachelorette party was called to be held there while Sobek was off *handling* something at his *work*. He was helping someone under his wing take a count of the number of fruit their *company* had imported to be mashed into different wines. Of course, no one but Lennena and Sadie in the room knew this. Sadie's and Sobek's grandmother, Cee, knew it as well, but she knew it in a way where she forgot and chose to not remember it. Men had done worser things, and bootlegging was making Sobek good money. He would assure Lennena, quite often, that he was merely building up savings for them and their future. It was as if they were *quietly* Cleopatra and Mark Antony. *Okay, sweetheart. Go out and conquer. I love you.*

The champagne flutes, their painted nails, alight below the chandelier. Unnecessary laughter flailed before the clinking glasses cheered. This regal room, its scarlet walls, where tassel-gowned women were loud and buzzed, almost mimicked dusty dungeons as Sadie almost shared a horror story. Sadie hid a horror story. Lennena's grin, a champagne sting, as spotless walls absorbed every rumor's breeze. But bliss began its dwindling as Sadie refused sharing that story. Sadie hid a horror story.

She was ready to share it, but not yet, not until everyone had their healthy amount of alcohol. She would tell it naturally then.

There were six women in the living room which was illuminated by the orange hue of a chandelier, and not any orange truth from the fireplace. That brick-toothed mouth was dormant. The windows were cracked to invite the merry musk of May into the room as second glasses of champagne were poured.

There was Sobek's and Sadie's grandma, Cee, and then three of Lennena's friends, Vicky, Esther and Polly. That trio in the flapper attire with bobbed hair and flaky-glimmering dresses seemed identical on account of the similar ways their faces absorbed the makeup, and in the identical way that the three of them mourned their empty packs once full of smokes. These three inherited themselves a crimson cushioned sofa as the walls of the room almost became brown in the dimness of night. Cee, Sadie and Lennena got their own chairs.

These three women on the couch were childhood friends of Lennena's, and had maintained the friendship through school. Her connection with them dwindled a little the more she said nothing about her tannish pantsuits she wore to the museum, the more she talked about her books she read, and the more the three women talked about the boys they met each night in the city. Around 1922 and 1923, they became heavy in the nightlife, adoring the swinging dances, cigarettes and strange men.

The Spanish Flu, the German bruise, had snatched their fathers all away. Promiscuously strutting to the deco clubs to fill their place. The suffrage dance, adrenaline left behind from marches on Boston street, surged through overconfident smirks, hiding next to trauma under tassels. Hiding trauma under tassels. Validation, from rousing men, for vague and drunk·invites to city castles. Becoming clean with strangers' sweat, ignoring their trauma under tassels. Hiding trauma under tassels.

Of course, men were up to *good old fun* as well. It was a group effort, but it was unnatural- unnatural to some. God forbid anyone have a coherent and reasonable opinion against it.

Esther, Polly and Vikcy dove into this life as Lennena preferred remaining in some kind of school-like setting.

This was when Lennena came across Sobek; someone whose face lit up to hear someone talk about things he found interesting. She knew a lot more than him. He enjoyed listening to her, almost learning something every time they talked in those early days. She loved how his face looked as she talked to him. It always looked as if he was *stupidly* listening, learning something important again.

Unaware to Lennena Bloo, Sobek had himself going in circles about one flapper, leading him to the conclusion that an *appropriate* woman was better company. He had decided to stay the bloody hell away from flappers, and found himself his angel.

So, the three flappers were bridesmaids as an ode to not only Lennena's past, but to their own. Though time had let them drift to different venues in life, even they had some respect for that in the black rimmed eyes. But the mascara caught as much human decency as it could, never letting anyone in. The only way to get close to going in was by going to the clubs, offering them cigarettes, and validating them about their looks.

"I must say," Cee began with that easy-going voice of hers, "it is absolutely refreshing to hang with a younger bunch."

She began to wrestle off a chuckle. "My mans has been giving me a run for my money."

Esther leaned forward on the sofa which held the three flappers, and uncapped her voice. "The men become a tougher lot ahead in age, do they?"

"No." Cee said as if that *no* deserved just a bit more time to be pondered about. "They just fall asleep a lot, and forget a lot."

"Sobek must have his grandpa's memory." Lennena joked.

"Aw, well." Cee chirped. "They remember the important things."

"They do." Lennena agreed, with the comet of a thought glossing then vanishing from her eyes.

"Oh, but everything is important." Polly chuckled. The six in the women casted their agreeing laughs into the dull and lightless fireplace like roses being thrown into a not yet closed coffin.

"How is the flapper life in Boston?" Lennena asked, to which it was Vicky who pricked the air with a voice all too used to shouting in clubs. "Luminous."

"Lennena! It's a ball!" The one named Esther exclaimed. "You ought to come smoke and dance with us sometime."

The trio clucked into a broken quartet of agreement, clucking to their silent friend.

"The live bands, Lenenna-" Esther sighed longingly, "-oh my goodness."

"Have you been anywhere in the city at night, Sadie?" One of the three asked. Sadie shrugged. "Every now and then."

Polly chirped, turning the trio's mascara bagged eyes to the bride. "Oh, you just ought to come, Lennena."

"Oh no." Lennena shook her head. "I'm busy with Sobek now-"

"Even married women need some fun. Right, Cee?" Vicky suggested. The grandma forced a polite nod.

Lennena bowed her head in defeat with a smile. "Fine. One night sometime. I'll come after him and I truly settle, and spend some good married time together."

"Bring Sobek." Cee suggested. Sadie began chuckling at some boondocks-style memory. "Grandma! He only dances when he drinks."

"Well." Cee pondered aloud. "Limit him to two, Lennena. That'll be enough, but, also, tell him that his grandma tells him to not be an idiot."

"I bet that'll also work coming from you, Lennena." Polly teased.

As the group tossed around differently toned chuckles, Lennena spent no time scanning the polished floorboards and dusty bricks of the fireplace. The memory flicked through her mind as her eyes became still before she spoke. "I-I don't believe I've had the pleasure of seeing him dance drunk."

"Hm." Sadie laughed. "Well, no one in this room has seen him dance sober."

Lennena could not help but let slip a smile as she brought all the laughter to murder with her confession like a soldier reporting something to Aphrodite. "I have. A slow dance. He asks me almost every night."

"To dance?" One of the flappers chirped. None of the three were as baffled as Sadie was while she blurted out. "He- he does?"

Lennena proudly nodded, maintaining that smile. "We have our favorite songs, and he's always so gentle."

"My brother asks you to slow dance..." Sadie crooned with disbelief. Lennena chuckled in that gracious intoxication of gratitude.

"He is a sweet boy." Cee said. "Throughout his teasing and messing... and he really loves messing with his grandma... he really is the sweetest boy."

"Girls," Lennena said, turning to the trio of flappers, "it's why I don't really wanna go dancing in the city. I only wanna dance with Sobek."

"Oh." Polly began with a sympathetic apology. "We didn't mean it like that at all, Lennena. We meant only with us, not strangers."

"Yes." Vicky smirked. "Save the strangers for me."

"And you really would like the music and live bands, Lennena." Esther jumped in, matching Polly's tone while Vicky kept a sly look of greed upon her smirk, thinking about that night-life.

"I guess," Lennena began, "Sobek won't be going anywhere."

"Especially after tomorrow." Cee laughed. "You go out with the girls, and he can visit his grandma. Like they say about the best things, it'll always be there tomorrow."

Lennena thought about how her and Sobek looked out into the vastness of the twinkling plains. That whimsical shade of lime was still haunting her so beautifully, and she loved how that felt, feeling like a phantom was warning her about the excitement of tomorrow. She ignored those rules, and loved the excitement.

"Unless it's champagne." Polly joked with her champagne flute raised in the air.

"Well!" Cee exclaimed, rowing her tone with the oars of genuine interest. "How's the museum treating you, Lennena?"

"Wonderfully." Lennena smiled. "I was lucky enough to work on the Nefertiti exhibit before this vacation for the wedding began. We had a school visit it, and they just all looked so wonderful while reading the plaques and everything. You'd really love it, Cee."

Cee released a thinking groan. "Nefertiti."

"And they asked the silliest questions, Cee." Lennena spoke with a voice belonging to the plains of grass from earlier. "A little boy asked who *he* was. I told him she was a queen."

Cee chuckled. "That's precious."

"So used to having male presidents." Polly groaned, rolling her eyes with only a little bit of comicalness behind her tone. "Men, especially men still learning, gotta know that all women are just as capable as men in everything."

"She's extremely interesting, with what we know so far." Lennena exclaimed, her voice leaping into an airy excitement. "It's golden knowing women ruled something like Egypt once."

"We still could." Polly suggested, then joked. "Come on, girls. We're going to Egypt."

Cee jumped in in a more serious tone. "Oh, I got a few tricks for that."

"Wait, Lennena." Vicky clucked. "Who else is coming tomorrow?"

It felt like an appropriate question.

"Sobek has a few interesting friends coming. He was really adamant about having that lot come by."

Lennena answered. At this, Cee and Sadie's faces became happily glum with the knowledge of knowing something the three flappers could never have guessed. Lennena continued, knowing it was a thing for Sobek. "They're just extremely close friends of his, girls. But, I suggest you stick to dancing with the men in Boston.

"Well," Cee chimed, "I'm sure everyone will be a pleasant lot tomorrow. It's a wedding after all. And my grandson wouldn't invite just any bloody egits to his wedding."

"I happened to have not met any of these bloody egits yet." Lennena crooned in a failed attempt of sounding comical, maintaining her polite smile. It came off as rude, but Sadie knew Lennena meant no harm. Sadie nodded, trying to salvage some bit of decency in the room. "Me neither."

Decency was unsalvageable when flappers were present as the lust for a party, for a crowd that wreaked of tobacco and lavender, steamed away from the grey bags hidden beneath their mascara.

Sadie, the maid of honor, went on after a little sigh escaped out from her mouth. "Don't worry, Lennena. I double-checked the list when we got home today. We're sitting pretty."

"We do have a list." Lennena said in her teachery museum voice. "It may get a little crowded, but we'll have fun tomorrow. The venue is massive, and just brilliant. It'll make the clubs in Boston look silly, girls. It's a brilliant inversion of outer-space. It's so massive, but not a shadow is allowed to lurk in it. Nothing black about it. It's marble, and-and like snow in the summer."

Esther croaked like a tired general before a division, speaking for herself and Vicky and Polly. "Well, if it's a ball, then us three will take turns getting married in order to have a row of wedding parties."

A guiltless and greedy grin unveiled itself across Vicky's lips. "We'll draw straws."

Lennena's laugh was a little forced as if she was trying to make a puppy go back to its home after going for a walk. It didn't want to comply, but it did, digging its claws against the driveway only to lose, and be yanked away.

Sadie was the only one who did not nod or raise her champagne flute in the fizz of agreement. A phone conversation from a week ago was haunting her... that pleaful voice... haunting her. And, she remembered how sternly she had told that woman, how she said it so warningly.

And so, as the bachelorette party jabbered out of conversation into the hour of 8 o'clock, Sadie watched her mind linger into the memory of that phone conversation a week ago.

She had answered the phone while everyone in the estate was off and on about their own rambling.

"Hello." Sadie said in her usual sing-song voice.

A fruity but timid voice awoke from the other end of the telephone. "Sadie?"

"Who is this?"

"Vannollia." The other voice said with an unhealthy amount of hope, but the oncoming silence became polluted with the crunchy tartar of guilt. Crunching amongst every breath that this Vannollia took from the air, the guilt, it made Sadie feel like she was taking to a prisoner.

"You got some nerve." Sadie declared. "Goodbye-"

"Is Sobek alright?"

Sadie paused. Her frustration puckered itself upon her lips as she thought. She kept the phone to her ear as if to wait for Vannollia to say something better. Sadie let no emotion corrupt her voice as she blurted. "He's better than ever actually."

Vannollia sounded shy. "R-really? Okay."

"Yes." Sadie said with a bit of pride. "He's getting married wicked soon. Next week. And, he's never been happier."

Silence.

"So, don't call back." Sadie said. "We want nothing to do with you, woman."

Silence. Goodness, that's what space must have sounded like. It was a nebulous silence, swallowing every word that Vannollia had ever heard Sobek speak.

"Listen, Sadie, I just-"

"Three years on, and you call to check on my brother?"

"I care about him." Vannollia peeped into the phone. She did not want her voice to shake, but it did.

"That's rich." Sadie said while fighting back an angry chuckle. "Tell that to him next time you're in Salem."

"Sadie-"

"What?"

"Who is he marrying?"

Someone who loves him." Sadie said. She had dropped the attitude because it felt illegal to speak with any hatred while speaking about Lennena Bloo.

Vannollia sniffled. "Wh-what's her name?"

"Lennena Bloo."

"Is she pretty?" Vannollia beggingly asked. It was her shaky tone that begged for some invisible answer. Timid. Her voice was wet and timid like a fruit who hated to be picked.

Sadie answered without any expression. "She's beautiful."

"Oh." Vannollia ribbitted with a damper voice now, unable to hide her sobbing tone over the telephone. "She is."

Annoyed that the woman was crying now, Sadie groaned in a protective *back-off* sort of groan. "You're not invited to Lennena Bloo's wedding."

"Is Sobek home?"

"No. He's out with her now. Helping her out at the museum. Gonna go now?"

"Bye, Sadie." Vannollia said weakly. "Would you tell him-"

"No. Absolutely not." Sadie said. She was unable to keep her chuckles dead. They arose like hungry zombies, grunting into the phone. "You've been dead to him for three years, you know? I swear, he's done everything in his power to forget your name."

Silence.

"Does he still work in the coal mines?"

Sadie crooned. "Now, why would you care?"

"I had a change of heart."

Silence again. Sadie must have been outraged because the cadence of her breath was a muffled flare behind closed lips against the telephone.

Vannollia hiccuped sob after sob, and Sadie just hung up.

So now, a week later, Sadie sat in the room with the bachelorette party. Her young eyes were glazed with the horror story of hearing Vannollia *sad.* She never knew that that woman could have emotions like that, or actually care for Sobek. No. Sadie knew that was a lie, and it made her grimace as the voices of Lennena, Cee and the flappers drivelled into the muffled muck of night.

"Everything alright, Sadie?" Lennena asked. Sadie nodded, responding. "Yeah, yeah. I'm just tired."

"Well!" Cee exclaimed. "I think we should all get some well-deserved rest for tomorrow."

"We should." Lennena agreed as the trio of flappers on the sofa sipped the final sips of their champagne. She stood up. "Come on, girls. There'll be plenty for you all to drink tomorrow."

***

Vannollia vesselled a frown with vanity. Before the mirror like a vampire imagining their old self, she pondered bout the cost of tickets taking folks to Salem-town. Yet a pale confidence aboard her face was its own ticket. Vannollia vesselled a frown with vanity, and she bought the ticket, boarding that adventure to the ceremony.

A week after her telephone conversation with Sadie, Vannollia had boarded the train from New York to Massachusetts on the morning before the day of the wedding. She was aboard the very train which crossed the lime colored horizon, chugging before the very eyes of Lennena, Sobek and Sadie, disrupting their ogling about the grass.

Around 3 o'clock in the afternoon, the train pulled into Back Bay Station. Wearing a blood-scarlet dress coat over a flapper's gown of red and a violet bonnet above her jet-black hair, Vannollia began rambling in search of a cab to Salem. Boston was not her style, and she preferred getting to Salem earlier than later. She had been in these towns and cities once, and found them to be shy oases of dirt compared to her New York.

Her glare was knitting that vintage apology. But she lit the quilt aflame while catching coffee in a cafe. It woke her up enough to let her know how *sorry* sounded fake. A nervous village burned behind her eyes without escapees. Her glare was killing that vintage apology. She sipped her coffee, all alone as Salem lingered deep into the day.

She thought about the hiccup-confession of love. It stung to think about how fake it felt escaping out her mouth. She lied about her loving Sobek back in 1921. Now before his wedding could begin tomorrow- Love awoke. She thought about the hiccup-confession of love. She thought about how every lie she ever told mimicked *I love you*'s sound.

"Thank you." Vannollia smiled at the waitress after she swooped to and past the table, picking up the pennies that Vannollia left over the little scrap of paper called the check. The realest smile, given to a waitress. It made Vannollia frown at the spot where the check and pennies used to lay, one atop the other.

Now, with her coffee almost finished, and the single cup paid for, she reached into a little purse she had brought and pulled out an old letter. It was dated back from February, 1921. Goodness, she forgot that month even existed. She reread the return address of the letter with eyes that excited themselves to read that boy's sloppy cursive again.

As the dying sun returned the town of Salem back to tannish curses, orange-warning hues of that almost deceased evening, Vannollia wondered when she should go see Sobek. That night? Or the wedding tomorrow. Her eyes argued with each other above the letter. After a sip of her cooling coffee, she told herself tomorrow. Just before the wedding, she'd tell him that she actually loved him. She missed him. She missed how he treated her. Missed his devotion. His commitment, which was so big that it almost became commitment from the both of them.

Why did the violins refuse to whine for her? All throughout her thinking, not a vein verdunned her disappointment as she thought about her and him celebrating down the church. That regret refused becoming readable against her face. Why did the violins refuse to whine for her? Her only instrument was a heart below an unsympathetic glare.

She missed how Sobek's heart rebelled distance for her. A daydream recalled how Sobek limped throughout the crowded ballroom, in a snow-colored suit with puppy-like eyes that escaped the pound. And those nervously in-love eyes pretended to not see her. She missed how his heart rebelled everything for her, even that rebellion he started against his own exploding nerves.

She bowed her head, and gathered her bearings while remembering the few days and nights she had with him three years ago.

Then she remembered his second trip to her, which sprouted from him saying *rent a castle with me, my love,* over the telephone in a breathless hush a hundred and a hundred miles away.

Before she could remember anything, she heard her wedding gift clink against her rose quartz crystal in her purse. She thought the bed of ancient romantic letters would have muffled that metallic kissing in her purse. The wedding gift... kissing the rose quartz; that pink, oval, crystal.

Nervous, she left the cafe.

After regrouping, and after battling old memories that nearly brought her to tears, she trotted into a tiny hotel nearby the old church she had once walked past when she was in Salem the last time. She couldn't cry. She didn't dare let herself observe how decrypted and rotten that appearance of the church had become. Her heart was already too busy looking at it for three years, wondering if she had made a mistake. She could not look at it. She couldn't cry. Her mascara looked too good for her to cry.

She was right after all, and Sobek was wrong. She'd forgive him this time.

Night had hanged itself outside the living room window, and that image of her indigo and paling feet was frozen against the glass. The muck of rooftops of Salem appeared as crusty toenails, pointing up to the shadow of the swinging corpse in the now completely withered gown-all black and blue. Everyone joined the funeral nap except for those in love. They stayed up until they collapsed.

Sobek had retired to this now empty living room in which the bridal party was sipping champagne and sharing chat a few hours ago. He and his business partner had taken a surplus count of bananas, and stowed it away in crates for some college-drop-outs from the northern boondocks to mash in the coming days. He had to trust in his partners as he would be away soon with Lennena for their honeymoon, but, as the events of the day fermented in his mind, he remained retired inside the living room. This was the final surplus after all, because he was done. His broken heart was healed, and it was time to find something sober to do for a living.

He was alone on that crimson cushioned sofa. The coffee table between him and the now blazing fireplace held a little red box on it. It was rectangular in shape with a warning written atop it in bold and black ink: **DON'T THROW OUT.** Its dormancy and silence seemed to match the angry crackling of the fire. It fitted well, and it was sobering to feel as if he was a cremation ceremony, about to throw something in a fire again. No. He was not going to throw the rest of himself inside any fire again, but his exhausted eyes sure hinted that this remained a major possibility.

He leaned forward. By the command of his tired but gentle fingers, the top of the box, which was tattooed with that ominous warning, was flipped back. The inside of the box was spacious, almost empty. The odor of burnt glass hit him after he reached the tips of his fingers into that miniature brightly crimson casket. He crumbled it all up into his hand, prying it out of an abyss of memories. The fire complimented his silent bravery as nothing burnt his hand. He felt the tiniest bits of rock-like bits press against the skin of his palm and fingers like the abandoned bones of an infant rodent. There was one large chunk amongst the grains of rock-like mystery. If he was blind, he would've thought he was holding rocks and sand, but his eyes were open when he threw the rose quartz crystal into the campfire three years ago.

His broken heart against the lines inside his hand. It's pieces like remnants from shattered galaxies; pale and jagged. He was looking at it like looking at poison in a chalice. Asleep upon his palm alike the corpses in no-man's land- his broken heart against the lines inside his hand. The dust and clumps of sharp and shattered pieces slept inside his closing hand.

After pondering, he shimmied the remnants of the burnt crystal back into the little red box and closed it.

That unblinking gaze adored to hide the truth, but now there was only one thing he knew. Not banana wine. Not memories from prison ships. Only her.

"How was your meeting with your *friend?*" Lennena chirped upon her entrance. Her smile seemed more real, but it was indiscernible if it was because of Sobek's presence or because someone had finally cast a match into the fireplace. The fire truly made the living room as vintage as a cave. It was the regallest one any caveman could own.

"He is a friend actually." Sobek explained. "A childhood friend. You've met him."

Lennena stood about two yards away from the company of the sofa, chairs and the coffee table. She clasped her arms together like a barmaid too excited for the ending of her shift, and she aimed a waiting glance against her groom. An effortless smile slipped across her lips, but it was too faint to notice in the dim room. All that was noticeable was how the orange haze from the fire radiated against her groom's face as the wafting scent of burning wood exhaled from the fireplace.

"What's on your mind?" Lennena asked. Her smile became more noticeable. It almost became as bright as the orange when Sobek chuckled and tilted his head towards her. He spoke with a smile. "Tomorrow."

"And the rest of our lives?"

"Tomorrow."

"I know." Lennena said. "I couldn't focus at all while everyone and your grandmother were in this room."

"How was that?"

"I couldn't focus." Lennena shrugged. That smile could have exploded then if she stopped trying to hide it.

Sobek gruffed, looking back to the fire. "Good, because I don't even remember what I did with my mate after our business."

"Ah-"

"And I'm sober. Sober and excited, Lennena."

"I had a little bit of champagne."

Sobek chuckled again.

"The girls had more than me." Lennena began in a teasing net of defensiveness. "Gotta keep them at ease somehow."

"My Lennena Bloo." Sobek sighed a sigh that told the world he wanted to slouch, but he remained sitting with good posture. "You could bring a hunting tiger to ease. Could bring any ancient god to ease."

Lennena's smile began to flicker after catching sight of that affable-red and tiny box. She nodded. "What's in your little red box?"

"Lennena." Sobek muttered as if he was about to confess something. "We're getting married tomorrow."

"Yes?" She chuckled, keeping her hands clasped. As if to play a part, she stiffened her posture and waited for her man's next line to be delivered on the stage.

"And well," Sobek said, "I need to give you something."

Her posture shrank, becoming calm again. Her gaze mimicked the twinkle that the fire held. It was as if she was seeing the little red box again.

"Goodness." She chuckled. "We already gave each other our rings."

"No, Lennena. What's in this box is more precious than any gold or diamonds to me. And, tonight, it's become all the more precious because I know I'm ready to give it away."

It was not a silence that entered the room then, but it was the ghosts who all politely left. Their absence was beautiful. Lennena Bloo and her Sobek became the only people on Earth.

"Here." Sobek hushed. "Sit."

Without hesitation, Lennena unclasped her hands and plummeted away from her standing position. She plopped next to him. A symphony of squeaking cushions began as the two bounced their bottoms up and sideways until their shoulders touched. They leaned on each other, and remained leaning on each other with the same fire being reflected in their eyes as the little red box watched them.

She watched a foreign nervousness contort his face alike a melting sculpture. Her angel gaze had fixed it just before it melted. She was there, and he was okay.

"I- I never thought I'd give my heart away again." Sobek began to confess, looking into the fire as Lennena looked at him, watching how his lips molded word after word.

"What do you mean?" She asked. Her eyes darted to the box again. "What's in the box, darling?"

Silence. He was busy thinking. He was busy trying not to remember something.

"Why are you nervous?"

"Lennena." Sobek said as his answer drained the noise from every thunder on the Earth so it could roll out of his lips as bluely beautiful as the cellos' boom behind the storms of summer. "My broken heart is in that box."

Lennena swivelled her eyes away from him and onto the box, reading its sloppily written warning aloud. "Don't throw out?"

"Three years ago- I had this crystal, right?"

"Yeah?"

Sobek continued, unaware about the half-cracked smile on his face. It appeared as if he was getting punched, and enjoying it while some vintage city-memory replayed only for him. "It was called a rose quartz. It was a pink colored crystal that represented love, and it supposedly had magical and romantic properties or something. It really was beautiful, like-like some pink mineral between diamond and- whatever."

Lennena chuckled. Hearing that boyish bloke become excited or nervous about something always made him look cuter to her. He seemed to be nervous and excited at the same time as he aimed a thousand-yard stare against the little red box as if he was happy to see his own corpse like a ghost before its own grave. He saw some strange chance to wake up in that box.

"It was just something that meant something to me once." Sobek explained. "But, three years ago, a few months after I got it, I threw it into a campfire."

"Why?"

"Doesn't matter." Sobek said in a quick tone with a nervous smile. He continued as that smile vanished quicker than it came. "But I salvaged the remnants of it when the fire died. Dug all the broken crystal pieces out from the ash with a stick. I collected it all, and, uh, I put it in this little red box."

Lennena spoke as if she was the only cloud in the warmest spring and night-time sky; the only cloud who got to watch the plains remain the beautifulest lime. "Don't throw out."

"And all these broken, shattered, pieces of crystal," Sobek explained almost as if he was talking to himself while staring at his little red box, "I call it my broken heart. And-for a wicked long time, I never thought someone could actually love me. But, this stupid part of me had one last sip of hope left, and that's why I kept my little red box all these years, Lennena. Always keeping hope and my broken heart in my little red box."

Lennena watched a tear begin to crawl down Sobek's face. It had its own crystal-clear color, and became orange in the firelight.

"A part of me always knew you'd come." Sobek's voice shook ever so slightly. It made the fire become a silent watcher, shying into that abyss of colder flames.

"Sobek." Lennena said. His hair was soft against her palm. She combed his hair back because she knew he liked it. She knew how it calmed him. She knew everything that calmed him.

Sobek whimpered. "You've proved you'll give my broken heart a home."

"Sobek."

"So," Sobek spoke in a soft hush, "this is your little red box now, Lennena. It belongs to you."

"Come here." Lennena begged.

Sobek twisted around and hugged Lennena. They fell against one another on the sofa. She hushed into his shoulder while his tears dampened her own shoulder. "I love you."

"I love you too." He said.

Their little red box watched them hug on the sofa.

After waiting a little to see if her Sobek was okay, Lennena spoke with delight amongst the sound of her voice. "You know," they slipped partly out of the hug to meet each other's eyes again, "I'm already imagining this little red box upon our nightstand in the house we bought for us."

They shared a smile without the need to chuckle, and without the need to check if the other one was smiling.

Lennena repeated that nebulously black and eternal phrase, using it to mention everything. "Don't throw out."

A pause began to die again.

"Sobek, what in the world can I give you now?"

"A kiss tomorrow." He answered with that face reddened below his ripped veil of tears. "After lifting ivory veils to meet my angel."

Their relieved smiles vanished in a kiss. They became resurrected after that farewell *smack* popped upon the separation of their lips. And then, their faint smiles had never looked newer.

"It was always meant for you, Lennena."

Lennena spoke with the softest cheering in the wake of their kiss. "You're already asking me with that stupid twinkle in your eyes, so, I'll ask first."

The happy contortion of his face, which rose his cheeks up, caused the tears to die away along his face.

"Sobek?" Lennena asked. "May I have this dance?"

"You may, Lennena Bloo."

"Our final dance before our wedding."

As Lennena stood up like a barmaid relieved from her shift, Sobek jabbered. "Lennena, you can always have every dance."

"Let's not let this last too long, darling." Lennena suggested after her eyes fluttered back and forth from a grandfather clock in the room. Its tired pendulum was outliving the fire in the fireplace.

Sobek stood up. The fiance and fiancee took each other into their dancing positions, slipping one hand over the other.

"Finish this dance before midnight. Before tomorrow." Lennena Bloo warned, exhuming myths from that relief about tomorrow. "Tomorrow begins all wicked soon, and it's horrible luck for us to see each other on our wedding day."

Lennena and Sobek picked an old vinyl record. A dead and lonely fireplace still remained with spitting embers, so, below the growling music, every lyric became re-verbed. That melody had distorted like an edit made by nymphs imprisoned in coal mines. Those earthly angels forgot what real music sounded like, so this grainy sound was lost, muffled and sounded underground. Lennena and Sobek swayed to old vinyl records. A'love alive inside the other's arms, against their chests, and kissing smirks.

She swayed a cautious way because of his bad leg. He never limped with that angel against the heart behind his chest, orbiting close with matching slowness like galaxies colliding. Tomorrow played a cautious violin before midnight's breath. She swayed a cautious way because of his bad leg with her fingers latched upon his shoulders, watched by the little red box.

"Lennena." Sobek hushed after his eyes darted from the grandfather clock then to his Lennena. "I really do wanna have our photos taken in the plains."

They continued swaying in the slowest pace around the scarlet walled abode like ghosts in an abandoned jail cell.

"Wouldn't it be wonderful to catch the whimsical twinkling green in color, keep it all green forever."

"Lennena." Sobek chuckled in a hush. "It'll be green forever. It's grass. Like the sun remains it's-"

"Lellow."

All Sobek could do was smile. He tried matching the volume of everything ambient about the night; the cold blackness outside, the dying fire, the crackling dust inside his little red box. "Like your golden and lellow blonde hair. You're my sun, and keep me the color of those fields."

"Green?"

"Alive."

Lennena never let the giggle escape her smile. She wanted that ability to hear his every word.

"Like the lellow sundress you wore when we met in the forest that day in the fall." Sobek said in a hushing tone which only told promises. "The lellow sun above our wedding day tomorrow. My love-" he broke into thankful laughter, "-we'll change our bedroom's wallpaper into lellow when we move in."

They nodded, agreeing with whispering chuckling as the rest of the world slept.

"You are my lellow everything, Lennena Bloo." Sobek promised. "No darker shade eclipses that heart in the little red box for you. Only lellow."

Lennena dropped her gaze so that it fell against her Sobek's shoes to watch how they wiggled next to hers. Both were softly shuffling almost with circular patterns during musical eavesdropping. Every note adored to spy upon them.

"Lennena."

Lennena raised her noggin, meeting Sobek's calming gaze above his smile which knew no reason in revealing teeth. He only smiled with that dumb sculpture of his lips. They always seemed fatter when he smiled like that.

"Yes, my Love?" Lennena chirped. She fixed her palm against his, tightening her grip as that melancholic happiness continued out of the gramophone. It was a jazzy tune, just slow enough for night.

"I also wanted to tell you," Sobek began with a nervous hiccup beggingly adventuring for an escape from his throat, "the bootlegging business is done for me."

Lennena smiled a smile of welcomed disbelief. "Is this true?"

"We counted all that we have left now, all has been sold, and nothing else will be made now." Sobek said. "We're done with that life, Lennena. You know, seeing you in the museum really inspired me-"

"Really?"

"And Imma start my studies to become a history teacher next year. I wanna teach history."

"Do you really?" Lennena smiled as if it was too good to be true. Sobek nodded. A bit of his black hair flopped out of place upon the final bob of that puppy-ish nod.

"All the leftover bananas are being sold to markets and sh-stuff." Sobek explained. "Final bottles are being shipped to Chicago."

"I'm proud of you, Sobek."

"Well, Lennena," Sobek said, finally cracking his smile open enough as his Love's voice plied it more open, "this is because of you."

"Now- Sobek." Lennena cooed with a bashful voice. She did not want to take credit because, deep down, in all the belief she had in him, she knew what he was capable of. She cleaned her smile with that adoring glimmer bout her eyes. "I mean it. I am proud of you."

It took a few breathless looks into her eyes, but Sobek responded with an honest acceptance. "Thank you."

Unmelting hands, his candle skin, gently holding Lennena Bloo. Exploratory meeting lips removed the noise from living rooms. The circle sway, their softest pace, became the chords for gramophones to learn. The static jazz mimicked their steps as they were watched by the little red box. Watched by Sobek's little red box. Her solar hair, her sunny stare, that the groom remained orbiting safely calm. The tartar of space disappeared as Lennena saved Sobek's broken heart, shattered in their little red box.

***

It was around 11:53 when a nebula of blackness lingered outside that estate. A plutonian warning married every streak of sableness amongst the sky. And, standing in the kitchen, Sadie looked against it all. She had changed into a scraggly nightgown. It was a pale and sickly shade of something in between the spring-time petals of white, green and yellow. In the drunken dead of night, no colors seemed to matter. But, she was nursing a candle on the kitchen counter. It flicked an orange song below the window. Steam began its swimming lessons in an upside-down dive as the young woman took enjoyment watching that declining brightness dim.

As she watched the wrinkles droop against the creamy pillar that propelled a dying wick against the near-midnight, she wondered bout her lack of sleep. She found a different kind of sleep amongst the dying body of candles; melting, melting, melting all as black nebulas lingered outside that estate as if the sun did not even exist.

"Boy! Your grandmother's a real catch, isn't she?" Polly crooned upon her brisk entrance into the kitchen. Her thin and winding body still remained inside her flapper dress. Night life had destroyed her circadian rhythm, but no exhaustion crept below her eyes. The kitchen proved its poor recognition of dresses like so as tassels made a jingle over every tile. It was the way that the tiles repeated every shimmy in a shy echo which told the kitchen that no flapper entered it before.

When Polly finished walking up to Sadie, that symphony died. She thought she heard a pale color of gold try speaking to her in the hum of silence that followed her steps.

"Can't sleep either?" Polly asked. Sadie nodded. That affable voice began its horror story. "I heard a ghost a week ago, crying over the telephone."

"Ah!" Polly's eyes alit themselves, welcoming starved mermaids below the fogged surface of gossip. "Who called?"

"Someone I shouldn't have answered." Sadie glummed. Her eyes began their odyssey out the kitchen window once more. She shook her head. "I just got a bad feeling about it. The voice reminded me about a time when my brother was in some pain."

"The prison ship?"

"That's the family secret." Sadie said half jokingly, but also half warningly. "If you ever brought it up, he'd never shut up about it until you gave the bloke a drink. He'd only tell you the stories he wants to tell of course."

"So, what pain?"

"Nothing. We're all over it now."

"It was heartbreak? Wasn't it?" Polly poked with coals releasing sparks of hot excitement in her whisper. "And he's over it too?"

"He is." Sadie moped. "Not me. No one treats my brother badly. I can tell he's been over it for a while because of how he looks at Lennena, you know."

"Ah. We'll see it tomorrow."

"And-" Sadie said, beginning to chuckle, "-you know he's gonna cry, right?"

"Aw. So sweet." Polly said with something fake about her tone. This, she was not ashamed of. Her mind remained upon the telephone call, the grudge which Sadie kept, and a broken-hearted boy. She continued in a more excited tone. "Who broke his heart?"

Cee entered in a nightgown that was more comically confusing than her granddaughter's. It was still cursed by some late decade from the 1800's, and it made her look a little bit more like a squash. Cee didn't care though.

It was comfy, even in May, and every night of every season was already impressed by her.

Sadie exclaimed. "Grandma?"

"What in the blooming world are you two doing up?" Cee asked. Sadie moped. "Just looking out this kitchen window."

Cee retorted. "As the sanest minds do at this hour. And what is it that we see?"

She shuffled to stand between the younger women, and the three now truly were looking out the kitchen window.

"Just our reflections." Sadie said. Polly wobbled her head as she looked for a way to fuel the still incubating friendship between her and Sadie. Polly said. "I see the foggy reflections of three queens."

Cee chuckled. She shuffled out the way, and searched for a water bottle in a cabinet. It was a glass bottle. She then retrieved a tiny glass, and poured herself a glass of water.

"We were about to talk about someone from Sobek's past." Polly said.

Some austere sort of dead regret began to wilt away from Sadie's face when she heard her grandmother cry a surprised gasp. "Sobek's past?"

"A week ago," Sadie began with a tired voice, "Vannollia called the house. Luckily, I was the one to answer and no one else."

"Vannollia?" Polly gasped against the name. It sounded vexed below foreboding curses, making night a little darker.

"Oh no!" Cee gasped with the most sincere disbelief. "Stop! When did she come out of the wood-work?"

"Who is Vannollia?" Polly asked. Sadie's voice became more tired when she answered. "Sobek's former girlfriend. They dated for around seven or eight months back in 1921."

"What happened?" Polly asked. Cee sipped her water while her granddaughter took the stage again, finally explaining the arrival of the ghost story that was in her eyes during the bachelorette party. "Well-"

"Oh." Cee said after a gulp. "She was just bloody rotten, that one."

"Vannollia..." Polly repeated, then asked. "What in the world did she do?"

"Be careful saying her name." Sadie warned. "Don't want the sky to get darker."

Astonished by the grimaces on the grandmother and granddaughter's faces, Polly gasped. "What in the blooming bloody Hell did this woman do?"

"Well," Cee shrugged, "I'm sure Sadie knows it better than I do."

"First of all," Sadie began, "he rarely ever talks about his problems to any of us. If I wasn't around to see all of this unfold, I wouldn't know about it. So, when he came to me about *somethings*... I knew it was tricky for him."

"You're really writing this out like it was a war, huh." Polly clucked. Cee agreed in her accent of exhaustion. "Oh, just cut straight to it, Sadie. We're getting tired."

"I need my gossip." Polly noted like someone about to light up a cigarette; focused on one thing. "But, be quiet because I know- I just absolutely know- that Vicky would drool over this."

"It was a long-distance relationship." Sadie continued. "Started back in December 1920, if I remember that right. Throughout those times, he always seemed a little extra happy on the first of every month. I think that was their *anniversary* of meeting. I don't know how they stumbled across one another with the distance and whatnot, but it was a romance of letters, poetry and telephone calls for months and months. Goodness, his voice was getting annoying. He called and they talked every single night. They talked about music and literature, and- I think- she really distracted him from getting lost again."

"Oh, of course." Cee nodded. "He was in love with her, Polly. Absolutely smitten."

"And, one day, in March," Sadie went on, "Sobek made the whole family tea. He sat us all down, held a family meeting and told us he was going to New York to meet the woman he loved."

"And you know, like we said, Polly." Cee said with a whimsical flail of her head, yanking a bit of comedic relief into the kitchen. "He was always a man of many words."

She had said that sarcastically. It made it difficult for Polly to imagine Sobek giving a speech about romance to his family. Hell, the most she ever heard from him when Lennena introduced them was a disinterested *what's up.*

"She lived in New York?" Polly asked, leaning forward and over arms she now crossed over her chest.

"Yup." Sadie nodded. "That is where the fella rambled to in early April that year. He spent some time there with her, came home with the stupidest smile on his face. He got a job in the coal mines to save up for a future with her. He told me he was planning on moving to New York by the end of that year to be with her. He sure was. He was working like a madman with that bloody bad leg of his. He would come home all sweaty and covered in the blackness from inside the caves, but he was happy because he ended those days with telephone calls from her. She always picked up too. Always talked to him."

Cee chimed in. "And it was celestial seriousness for our Sobek. He even told me about her. Honestly, all about the woman. That bloody wretch of a woman."

"Wretch?" Polly repeated with a worried tone. No worried tone matched the excitement in her eyes.

There was a pause in the kitchen as if the granddaughter and grandmother were debating who should say it.

Sadie took the floor, though she wished she hadn't. "She was a harlot apparently. While her boyfriend was in the coal mines, working, while he was slaving over his desk with love poems... she was getting railed for own money."

There was a silence that allowed an ending for the story, but it didn't end. Sadie continued. "There was a string of arguments via the telephone after that, but he forgave her. They decided to work it out, and agreed to keep trying with the relationship. June arrived and he was aboard a train again, racing to go see her a couple days and nights."

"It was after that when he started asking her to come here for once, right?" Cee asked. Sadie nodded, replying. "She refused. Said she was busy, and ordered him to stop asking. And no matter how many excuses she threw at him, he always shovelled him and his bad leg back into the mines to work for their future."

"Poor man." Polly said, thinking that the story was about to end.

"Now, in early July," Sadie continued, "Sobek got wind that Vannollia was in Salem to shop and see some cafes and whatnot. I went into Salem with him, because I could tell he was a little angry. He buried it all down though. I watched them stand before this wicked old-looking church. He was asking her to come meet the family, come for tea, stay. She refused. They kissed. She walked away. The part that hurt me was how I heard her tell him she loved him before walking away. And I saw my brother standing there alone, married to all that false hope Vannollia had been pumping into him for eight months."

"And," Cee jumped in, "he forgave her again."

"She was six minutes away from this very house. Didn't even wanna come by for tea. She stayed in some hotel that night in Salem. Left the following afternoon." Sadie groaned. "It hurt him. Our mum couldn't even get a word out of him for two days, crying in his bedroom while his girlfriend shopped six minutes away."

Cee bowed her head as the thought of her grandbaby being in that emotional pain was pulling tears away from her eyes. She sniffled. "I'm sorry."

"Aw, Grandma." Sadie hushed, hugging her grandmother. With a hint of bravery freshening the kitchen, Cee spoke. "And this is why we love Lennena. We see how she treats him."

Sadie nodded. "I swear, he was beginning to think men just didn't get loved in relationships. Then Lennena Bloo literally fell from *Heaven,* and saved him."

"When'd he and Vannollia end?" Polly asked, to which Sadie answered with a sigh. "Well, after the Salem incident, they argued on the telephone for weeks. He kept trying to salvage the relationship until she broke it all off. She told him she never loved him, even after all the times she said she did. It ruined my brother, Polly."

"I was with him when he burnt the letters and photographs. He burned everything." Cee recollected. "And not a tear trickled down his face as he watched everything shrivel in the fire. Stone-cold. Sullen. He watched it burn."

Sadie nodded, afraid to look at anyone else in the room. "He wasn't able to cry for months afterwards. He was so hurt that absolutely no tears dampened his face. After the breakup is when he began making banana wine... for obvious reasons."

"But," Cee began, "the morning after he burned it all, we went to the beach and stood in the water. I told him he was a beautiful person. He opened up to me a little then, and told me about the relationship. Now, I told him that she wasn't right at all. It helped for him to hear that he deserves someone who loved him. I think he was beginning to think that love was something that hurts. And what Sadie said, he was just requestioning a lot of things."

A silence came and went in the kitchen.

"Two years later," Sadie began with a smile, "he met Lennena Bloo. She saved our Sobek."

Polly listened. Her widened eyes forgot this was gossip. She was interested in a proper manner now as Cee nodded while speaking. "We know he talks to her. We know he's safe with her."

"But," Sadie chimed in, "we know there's one thing he's never told her. Never will tell her."

Polly frowned. "Vannollia."

Cee nodded. "He won't put that on her. And, he's past it now."

"I used to think no one would be good for my brother after that," said Sadie, "but Lennena came. He let her in. And look about tomorrow."

***

The dream became vivid again in sleep… always returning like memories do… the dream became vivid again in sleep.

And it made them remember it when they woke up.

A cruising gust exited dusk, dressed with tattered indigo silk. Octobuary windy musk exited out from Gallows Hill. The unseen ghosts, the rooftop guests, all were dancing merrily below this as frozen clouds rebrewed the past all stewing nothing blonde about the night. With nothing blonde about the night. The lampposts paled, 3 o'clock wailed squeals with warning curses that annoyed the pines. The tattered gown, a zombie flailed, frozen with nothing blonde about the night. With nothing blonde about the night.

Vannollia woke up in the Salem hotel room. Only she ruled one pillow, and ruled it so alone as the little bedroom was an indigo shade of darkness. It was the weird and rotting lie of 3 o'clock in the morning, and she hated how it glazed the ending of the old memory she had been dreaming about. The dream took a timid start before the night even began knocking on their hotel window. That was before it took its withering orange gown to trick or treat at other houses, mansions and apartment complexes.

Sitting up in the bed, she remembered how she told her closest friend how she did not belong in the prison ship arms of love. Such a phrase aged like the austere wine which was aging in a cottage in the woods of Lynn far away. That hypnotizing yellow darkness, like being the last bit of pulp inside a bottle of banana wine, haunted her as she wrestled with her memories.

Precious Love allowed itself into her mailbox. His precious ways to call her beautiful had never ceased in ink. She witnessed flames exit his heart, like a never shrivelling wick, and that was curing every angst and sorrow haunting her days. Precious Love will stay inside her padlocked mailbox. She loved his letters. Did she him? But she loved the way she caught his heart.

She began to cry.

A part of her did not feel about what he called her mistakes. She was just living her life the way she wanted to live it; free. She regretted losing him, letting him go, and that is what hurt in this 3 o'clock hour of early morning.

As the memory wept away into some sort of childish acceptance, Vannollia took the rose quartz out of her purse. She plopped onto the bed, pushing her back into the melodramatic happiness of memory that made her feel heavy below the tiniest of oval rocks. It was smooth against her fingers. It was more forgiving than he was whenever she did something he didn't like, didn't agree with. And that always happened, so, of course she left him.

Cafe moments, the train's movements, melted back through old memories. Observatory student pens ignored the stars for vintage scenes. With gentle palms, she held it calm, keeping that crystal inside her fingers. Smiling at the few April days, unaware about his little red box. Unaware about his red box. Without a frown, she propped it down, on the silk upon her chest above her heart. Anniversary wishes drowned, unaware about his little red box. Unaware about his red box.

Holding rose quartz, grin remorseless, recalling only every laugh. Disorientary heart's curses- she rarely tried to love him back. But his support, his love letters, was a faithful ticking in her mailbox. That affection never weakened. She knew she should have never let him go. She should have never let him go. The breath of her phantom interest, coming like a dove, and leaving like a crow on romance's cottage fences. She knew she should have never let him go. She should have never let him go.

Was she loving? Was she loyal? Did she start any arguments? An ordinary rapunzel- did she wear her hair down for him? A twisting gut, it's pleaful *what,* feeling sick beneath the rose quartz crystal. The memories battled questions. Did she help him forget Vannollia? Could he forget Vannollia? With daydream bells, a snowfall-veil, hid her face above her gown's magnolia. A ceremony apparel, would it help him forget Vannollia? Could he forget Vannollia?

***

Sobek woke up around 6 in the morning. The absence of his little red box haunted his room. It always felt as if something was missing from there since he became an *adult,* but his own heart was gone now. For three years, he had kept it beside his sleeping self. The red box would watch him sleep. It sat there like a lighthouse, silently swaying its scarlet hue in search of an angel to come and excavate the remnants of burnt rose quartz from inside. It was many times he took the biggest remnant out to hold it and think. He would study the pale and jagged nature of it, seeing something about himself in its sharp and rigid nature. He didn't have to anymore, but as he slumped up on his bed that morning, he felt as if something more was missing.

After waking up a bit, he remembered it was his wedding day. It was sunny, even for the hour. There were no brides stuck in the chimney. He was alive. Everything was good, so he got up to make himself a cup of tea while trying to ignore the absence of his little red box from his room.

There was a balcony on the third floor of the estate. He had his tea there while Salem woke up below the orange glare of solar explanations while the questions of night forgot what they asked. As he felt a strange breeze yank his earlier mood away, he realized that feeling of missing something was just him waking up. There was no absence in his room. His heart, his little red box, was with its home right then, beside Lennena Bloo as she slept like an oblivious princess after the fairytale ended.

Her flattened bun, its lemon mound, beneath a bonnet white as milk. Probationary giggles howled as bridesmaids praised the dress's silk. Blizzard laces, knitted mazes of frozen sugar down her shoulders' skin. Her gliding hands unwrinkled threads all as the polar dress polished her chills. The polar dress polished her chills. Unmelting shade, a dove surface, with the diamond pawprints arctic foxes quilled. The winter slept against her flesh all as the polar dress polished her chills. The polar dress polished her chills.

The pinkened splints, rescuing lips, that had expelled his trust issues, watched Aphrodite formed by nymphs, reflected in the mirror's suit. Prodding fingers, smoothing wrinkles, elegant like they held their cigarettes. Tucking fabrics back into place, keeping her lemon hair forever ripe. Her lemon hair forever ripe. Rebelling hair's thin pleaful hands- lellow reaching out the bonnet's cap of white. Superlunary lellow strands, keeping her lemon hair forever ripe. Her lemon hair forever ripe.

"You look absolutely stunning." Sadie sighed. The lobby of the dress shop was a silent and sleepy shade of white. Like unbrushed ivory, tan from age, the spacious lobby felt imprisoned in the dusty shade which haunts empty libraries; the color no one gets to remember. This austere and celestial expression of rotting white was similar to the shade of tea with too much milk poured in it, and the color was a dusty mist upon everything except the white gown she wore in front of the mirror.

The four nymphs in lellow dresses agreed with one another, marvelling at the bride. She truly was beautiful as something about the white bonnet, covering and hiding her lemon hair, made her seem ready to explore the coldness of outer-space.

"Goodness." Polly sighed, drooping her shoulders without enough energy to shrug. "Now *I* wanna get married."

"You're your own solar odyssey, aye?" Sadie chirped with a smile. A foreign bit of pride haunted her smile as she looked at her soon to be sister-in-law. No one knew how relieved she felt that it was Lennena Bloo.

"You belong in a museum of beauty, Lennena." Esther tried complimenting her. Disinterest plagued her voice as if she was missing something; lost in the neon gold of Boston nightclubs.

Lennena let her breathless voice escape against the mirror. "It feels like I'm in one."

While smoothing out the dress by snowmobiling their palms down her side, Vicky and Esther aimed curious glances at the mirror. They searched for a flicker of hesitation to comet through the bride's eyes, but they remained a solar shield. Anything negative that entered the atmosphere of her eyes burned up immediately, becoming dust. The two young women seemed to not understand as their looks of amazement were misplaced, placed on them for the wrong reason.

Polly had a guilty look on her face, knowing she was hiding something as that austere name vined across the wrinkles of her thoughts. It expanded, growling all as she helped the bridesmaids smooth out Lennena Bloo's wedding gown.

"You are magnificent, Lennena." Polly moped, dragging her hands away from that ambient and winter shade of Lennena Bloo's wedding dress.

"Thank you."

"I see," Sadie droned off with her usual disinterested and tired tone, "you got your bags all packed for the honeymoon."

"Yes." Lennena said, trying not to smile. She thought it was weird to smile as much as she had been.

Satisfied with her reflection, she broke away from the party of yellow that seemed to have been formed from some kind of lingering April breath. Those dandelions whispered her farewell while watching her stride off to a company of slouching suitcases and duffle bags against a wall that appeared duller in shade more than the others, which were an ivory shade of envy. That white-petalled wonder of the things that were white that morning were whimsical audience members. It made her feel embarrassed throughout her little stroll to her bags, who comically didn't care about anything. She felt watched by everything as her bridesmaids at least had the manners to pretend they were focusing on something else.

Polly and Sadie watched Lennena opened and reach into one of the duffle bags, retrieving a little red box out of it the way one may rescue an infant puppy out of a glass container.

"I've been seeing that in his room for years." Sadie muttered with a subtle sense of sentiment.

"Really?" Lennena asked, running her thumb over the surface which beheld the warning: **DON'T THROW OUT**.

"For a while." Sadie lifted her chin, unable to let her eyes draw themselves away from the gentle peace the little red box appeared to be in while held by Lennena Bloo.

"That was in his room? He gave it to you." Vicky jumped in after she finished checking how her reflection looked. "What's in it?"

Lennena shook her head and answered with her eyes remaining on the little red box. "It's private."

She sighed. It appeared she didn't wanna put the box away at all, nor open it in front of the bridal party.

"It's obviously something important." Vicky huffed, implying to the title on the box.

Sadie had a look of knowing on her face, guilty knowing. She agreed with a glum expression. "It is. Whatever it is, girls, it's safe with Lennena, and we should get back to getting ready."

"I am ready." Vicky said.

"The motorcoach should be here soon." Sadie sighed. "Do you want help with your bags, Lennena?"

"I-I'll carry this one." Lennena gestured to the bag which she retrieved the little red box from.

"Come on, girls. Grab a bag." Sadie suggested. Polly complied. Vicky complied in a tired way. Esther complied in an even more tired way, anxious for the ceremony.

Chatty murmurs drowned down the hallway as the bridesmaids hauled some luggage away, leaving Lennena Bloo alone in front of the mirror.

Confident in being alone, she flipped the box open, revealing the remnants of dusty grit inside. Like an archaeologist discovering a lonely firepit in a cave, she watched the shy layer of pink dust, gritty sand-like and flamingo colored pebbles, bow to the major piece of Sobek's broken heart. The pale and jagged rock, pale, it was the most sorry looking object she had ever seen, but it made her feel like she owned her own secret museum. It was not a smile on her face as she scanned the toothy terrain of the burnt rose quartz, but humbleness, gratitude, and peace.

A trust flared in her eyes, whipping away from her pupils in glimmering bursts, sending down radiation to the obscure appearing crystal. So sharp, edged and sick inside its broken shading of pink, it did not even know what shape it was supposed to be, but her solar eyes loved it all the same.

Unbeknownst to the bridal party, unbeknownst to anyone really, Sobek decided not to look at his reflection in any mirror. He let the oldest church in Salem see his wedding suit.

He hauled himself to spot where Vannollia kissed him three years ago, by that black fence, below one eavesdropping oak tree, near a blue house, in front of everything that tried hiding that stone-bricked and castle-like tower of the church. That place, it was the place where she showed him how a man gets loved in the world, when she walked away to shop. The hindsight made him feel foolish like a miner in a tunnel full of only mud, and no profitable ore.

He stood there in his oyster colored suit with the pink tie, ready for the wedding, but he almost felt that white shirt return upon his skin. He almost felt that hat, which Vannollia hated, materialize upon his scruff of black hair. No other memory had ever made him feel so lost before.

He remembered how stupid, how stupidly hopeful, he was back then. Every kiss was naive. Every understandment was gullible, and he truly was the puppy chasing its tail in that romance.

The sable bricks recalled the witch whose vex remained upon the lawn. Cruciblary curses ticked, keeping every blade of grass brown. "I love you too." She ran away, and left behind her violet colored voice to haunt and own him forever with final lies eroding Salem's church. Her lie eroded Salem's church. Its castle bricks, its waiting tint, it turned to stone because he believed her. As Vannollia wilted him, her final lie eroded Salem's church. Her lie eroded Salem's church.

Funeral grey, the church's shade. It matched the groom's beluga suit. Residuary romance sang alike a mourning whaler's tune. The hanging scene, its floppy feet never fleeing out of the church's sight. His awe rewatched their final hug with her mark on him eroding never. Her phantom eroding never. The court of time recalled his whine upon returning home after seeing her. Refusinary every time with her grasp on him eroding never. Her phantom eroding never.

Reverbed silence verdunned his breath, muffling his evicted hope. Parliamentary charcoal vests constricted every word he spoke. A viper hiss, the hurt he missed, vivid amongst the church's sable walls, eavesdropped upon his violent hush as Sobek told the past about his bride. He told the past about his bride. Voiceless vespers' vixen vapor that the voracious harlot had left behind, vanished in the church forever as Sobek told the past about his bride. He told the past about his bride.

"She loves me." Sobek closed his eyes, gritted his teeth and craned his neck. He snarled again, thinking about her lemon colored hair that put the neon hush of banana peels to shame. "She *loves* me."

He did not care about those who may be passing by on their way to work. Something seemed normal about a suited man standing before a church in the morning, but nothing felt normal to Sobek about that church, about how that three year old memory still verdunned its grounds, its brown lawn, its jetblack fence, its castle-like bell tower, and its medieval attire.

A little proud, a little sore, he scanned the stained-rainbow windows, astronomicly searching for a little good inside black holes.

He found nothing useful in looking in the past, especially as he stood in it, but he felt better to have done so. She felt cast out of him now, and that introspective exorcism was complete. He walked away from the black fence, feeling lighter, feeling free, and feeling ready to marry Lennena Bloo.

As he walked the short walk to the church of the wedding, he welcomed the image of the twinkling fields of lime colored grass in his mind. It lathered that whimsical green over the memory of the dead grass before the oldest the church in Salem. The thought was a yawning pair of scissors, snipping the strings that once kept him tethered to darker things. He shook his cuffs, flailing his wrists as he turned a corner.

The oldest church in Salem would never see him again.

Sobek had a pleasant march through the town. It ended when he got to the newer church. Its reddish bricks welcomed him, swallowing him in to see a room of empty pews. He figured the benches and pews must have been made of spruce wood, for they made the church seem wet and dark as some whimsically eternal night illuminated the obtuse lobby of the church. The palettes of the stained-glass windows seemed to be like watchful figures with hoods and cloaks made of rainbows from outer-space. Their guarding shine casted something from unexplored oases into the church. He walked through it all, walking towards a door in the back of the church that would take him to the basement.

The restrooms in the basement of the church were spacious, and the absence of a crowd upstairs made it all the more hauntingly silent. The green stall-walls, and their artificial-kiwi shade, made the room of waste alike a liminal space. No exit allowed itself to be visible amongst the sinks, mirrors and urinals. In that moment, only two people inhabited the entire church as the bridal party had not yer arrived, the wedding staff was outside to talk with the rest of the groomsmen, and family and friends were getting ready in their abodes and hotel rooms.

Only two people lingered in the church, below the floor of pews and stained-glass windows. Sobek and his best man, an Irishman named McKee, stood before the mirrors to fix their collars and ties. McKee's tie was yellow, while the groom's was pink. Their suits were a slick demanding shade of grey, and it made the greenness of the restroom seem like a fruit that would never become ripe; forever stale, never picked, ruined by someone else's sable suit.

McKee was a little bit more pale than the groom, but his fingers that adored to pluck the strings upon a guitar made him seem adorable in that grey suit, for he unsteadily tapped them on his pants. He was hammering and pulling the strings of his thoughts with a tune of second-hand nervousness. His brown and spiky hair was short, having seen a haircut a few days ago, but he still had the same widened look that Sobek used to see in the prison ship week after week.

"No whiskey until the night, McKee." Sobek declared. He was the one pacing now as McKee did a jig before the mirror to hype himself up. "You may fancy one of the bridesmaids."

"Oh, buddy." McKee spoke in that typical soft voice of his; soft and caring, but excited. "Don't worry. I'm sticking to the wine tonight. Are you nervous?"

Sobek stopped pacing and shook his head. "That's my best friend Imma marry today, McKee."

A silence came in the restroom.

"I always tell the others too," Sobek said with a promise exploding in his throat as if some memory was making him proud and somber all at once, "there's an angel for every one of us. She found me, McKee. Mine found me."

"Well." McKee sighed happily without the smile to prove it. He turned around and faced the groom. "I'm happy for you, man."

"Thanks, brother."

"Got an escape plan?"

"Shut up." Sobek chuckled. He forgot which leg had the limp as he shuffled up to McKee in front of the row of mirrors.

"Man," Sobek said with a smile, "I can't believe I'm getting married. I'm actually getting married."

McKee patted Sobek's shoulder.

"Anyone else coming from-"

"I invited all of them, McKee." Sobek said. "The ones whose addresses I have. God knows all their mailboxes got an invite before anyone else I know."

McKee hushed, agreeing with a somber silence that wanted to return into the restroom. "The way it goes."

"Aye." Sobek said with raising eyebrows. "Not the day for that. It's my wedding, huh."

"Yeah, man."

"Today," Sobek stated as he too looked into the mirror, "we celebrate love, McKee."

The muffled click of something opening came and went.

"I think that's one of the guys. I'll go see what they need, man." McKee said. Sobek nodded as if to agree that was an idea.

"Meet me outside in a bit?" McKee asked, skidding to a halt in the doorway. Sobek nodded again.

McKee exited, and Sobek turned back to the mirror, alone in the restroom in the basement of the old church.

The time was ticking like a sorry piano. The groom allowed himself to take a break before the mirror's view. Alone, he fixed his collar, tie and cuffs inside the church restroom. Would Lennena Bloo adore his sable suit before the kiss? And time was ticking like a sorry piano when the warning song of tapping heels arrived with that metallic echo.

"Congratulations." A shy and fruity voice moped. It was sincere, and the shyness about it made it feel all the more sincere as the sickly green walls of the stalls absorbed her voice.

Sobek craned his neck away from the sink, raising his head to the mirror. It was astonishing how calm he appeared when he saw what the mirror reflected. He did not dare turn around to see if it was real though.

He looked over his reflection's shoulder to see Vannollia behind him. Her flawless face adored no pimples. Her lips were puckered in an unsure frown of *hello* as the darkest red lipstick clung to every crack in her lips. Her short hair was bobbed back by her silver tiara. And everything unyellow and bloody-red about her was topped off by that scarlet gown wrapping her up. It exaggerated her figure in the distance between Sobek's back and the restroom doorway.

"Sobek?"

He did not say anything. He could have been considered paralyzed was it not for the shakiness of his breath. He barely even blinked as he just stared at her reflection.

"Aren't you going to talk to me?" She asked with a shy defeat about her soft voice like the grape begging not to be mashed into wine.

Sobek huffed to himself, still looking at her reflection. "A silly hallucination on my wedding day."

"What?"

"You're just a ghost." Sobek noted, determined. "You can't hurt me anymore."

He remained sullen, huffing in his grey suit while watching the glossy face behind his shoulder scrunch up. She was getting ready to fight back tears with that wincing face.

"I told myself you died three years ago." Sobek spoke to himself, still looking at her. "You're dead, and you've been dead for three years."

He sounded confident as if he was speaking to a stranded part of his reflection.

"Sobek."

"Whatever part of me you are."

"I'm still a part of you?" Vannollia crooned in a shy attempt of hope. Her rising cheeks became glazed with rivering tears when Sobek hushed. "You're dead to me. Hallucination. Ghost. I don't care whatever this is... I want you to leave."

"I've always been a part of you?" She asked through the rattling of hiccuping sobs. "Sobek, I just wanted to say congratulations."

"I don't wanna hear congratulations." Sobek demanded. That mirror should have shattered with the way his eyes stabbed her reflection. "I wanna hear goodbye."

"Have I always been a pa-part of you?"

"There hasn't been a day where I haven't thought about you, Vannollia."

Hope flew across Vannollia's eyes like a comet. Hope became a sparkling thing behind her contacts of tears.

Sobek continued. "But then I remembered how you treated me, so I started telling myself you died. I'm convinced it's true because your memory morphed into a phantom... never leaving me alone."

Vannollia's face morphed into a hysterical display of pain, wet pain upon her pale face. "What?" *What* was a pitiful squeal.

"Now," Sobek continued, "you're just a ghost. A hallucination. Saying goodbye to me on my wedding day. This part of me finally forever departing from me."

"Does she treat you well?"

"I'm not gonna tell you anything about her."

"Sobek."

"Go away." Sobek growled.

"Sobek, please." Vannollia begged, choking through her sobs. "Are you happy?"

Sobek stared deep into the mirror, studying how Vannollia's reflection broke out in tears. Three years ago that sight would have killed him. He felt nothing.

"Are-are you ha-happy, Sobek?"

He crumbled into the sink below the mirror. Burying his face into his elbows, he held the back of his head as if to not let any other apparitions and hallucinations escape his mind. He gripped his hair, ruining how he had combed it.

"Please," he grumbled in a growl that belongs in prison ships, "leave me alone."

That apologetic and sickly shade of green observed how Vannollia cried throughout the moment of silence. She sniffled.

"It's me, Sobek. I'm not a ghost." Vannollia pleaded. Her voice was wet, slipping in the purple puddle of hope. "Please. Turn around. Let me see your eyes one last time."

Vannollia watched Sobek's back shake as a little muffled sob punched the sink. It was drier than her own, but it hurt to hear. It had brought a brief pause to her own crying.

She gulped, ready to take a step towards the crying groom as he kept his head buried in the sink. "I could come over and t-touch you."

"Please-"

"I love you." Vannollia confessed. "I'm sorry I was a monster."

Earth could have stopped orbiting around the sun just then until Sobek remembered how she told him that in front of Salem's oldest church three years ago. It was a lie then. She told him so. She never loved him. She said it to appease him, to keep him. He remembered how she said it over the phone. How it sounded like a mercy killing, like releasing a dog in the middle of winter during a blizzard.

Without a word, his mind reversed and brought him back to cushioned seats. Unforebidingly, windows blurred the passing April scenery. A suitcase slept. His eyes unlocked as out the windows buildings woke and stretched before the lonely passenger- the naive idiot aboard the train. The idiot aboard the train. The chugging shouts, excited pouts, welcomed by exhausted twisting cityscapes. Involuntary gullible- the naive idiot aboard the train. The idiot aboard the train.

The whispers that began against the sink alarmed her, and it stopped her in her tracks. Her eyes began to bulge amongst the rivers of melted mascara as she listened.

Shaking shoulders, Sobek shuddered his forehead against the faucet. Malfunctionally frowns thundered, turning that expression scarlet. His mute exhales goosebumped the stall as he tucked himself below the mirror, verdunned with confusing flashbacks as hope began to wander down the drain. Her hope escaping down the drain. The corpse of second chances sank like a lifeless puppet drowning down a lake. With muffled sobs against his hands, their hope began to wander down the drain. Her hope escaping down the drain.

Sobek growled to himself, slowly sounding more angry the more he groaned into the sink. "This absurd hallucination. I can't trust my own mind. I can't trust- I couldn't trust anyone for so long. I didn't believe Lennena the first few times she said she loved me. I co-couldn't trust anyone-"

Sobek twisted around, exploding. "BECAUSE OF YOU!"

Vannollia flinched. Her mouth dropped, and she began taking backwards steps towards the doorway upon seeing how the man's twitchy face was beat-red, glossed in tears.

"I mean it this time." Vannollia promised, horrified by how ugly Sobek's face became in anger. "I love you. I will always love you."

He aimed a violent disbelief against her eyes. She aimed nothing back but the apology that became immortal in that moment.

"I-I'm sorry." She shrugged. It sounded insincere, but she was nervous, and shy in front of the heart she broke. And his hateful eyes told her she'd broken it forever, for he forgot about Lennena Bloo in the moment when she uttered her appeasing lie again. "Sobek, I *love* you. I love you this time."

Sobek paused. Vannollia was brave to remain standing before him. Her chest heaved, contrasting and expanding as her parted lips waited.

"Sobek," Vannollia took a step forward, shaking her head in a frantic manner as she plopped her wet voice into the restroom, "no matter who I was with, I was thinking about you the whole time. I n-never loved any of them. It was just-"

"Get out."

"Sobek."

Vannollia caught one more look of the scar she inflicted behind the man's eyes as he began refusing to look back at her. His eyes preferred the polished tiles of the bathroom floor then. He appeared so distraught that prisoners on death row may have been more well-kept together.

"Did you burn all my letters like I asked you to?" Sobek gruffed. There was a hesitance in his voice that made Vannollia question if he actually wanted to know the answer.

She shook her hand. "They're in my bag. Every single one of them, Sobek. With the rose quartz-"

"I asked you to burn my letters." He quoted himself flatly. He forced his eyes to verdunn Vannollia with the muddy grit he felt in the trenches of the heartbreak she inflicted. She saw it- how he must have stumbled after everything.

He muttered in a way as if his voice had a limp as well. "You brought your rose quartz?"

Vannollia nodded.

Sobek felt a foreign stake explode through his heart, sending a ripple of dullness into his stomach as if an unknown part of him was punched. His emotions kept his reddened face in an eternal wince as he squinted at the flapper in front of him, annoyed about the hope in her eyes.

He muttered. "I threw mine-" he hesitated, took a deep breath, and continued, "-into a campfire at my aunts."

He lifted his eyebrows as if he was proud of himself for it. "Didn't even cry, Vannollia. It lost its pink color. It shattered, and now it's just a pale and jagged rock."

Vannollia wanted to tell him she hated him, but she did not. She hated *why* he did that.

"I burnt the photos of us. Our letters." Sobek said as if it was a promise. He was becoming proud the more he snarled. "I burned it all, Vannollia, because I know-because-"

"Because of me." She moped, disappointed. She backed further towards the doorway. "I'll always love you.

Sobek turned back around to cry in front of the mirror. She was gone before his forehead even married his palms again.

And the groom began to crumble in the restroom. Crouching, fearing that apparition appearing past his shoulder, he dug his face against his palms as nothing else punched the mirrors. He didn't want to see another ghost of Vannollia as his joy began to crumble in the restroom. Alone, nobody saw the groom begin to cry in his sable, grey, suit.

The rainbow stained-glass windows watched mascara melt. Vannollia hauled herself across the aisle alone while crying, dreaming bout a wedding cake with blood to stain its creamy icing. Fingertips began to bathe a bullet in Holy Water. The rainbow stained-glass windows watched mascara melt, but nobody saw her baptize the bullet's brass as all her love ran out.

She heard his muffled cry as she bathed the bullet. Every squeak and squeal became a beat for splashing Holy Water. It was a song about resurrections out of the revolver. Her frantic fingers played their dampened notes against the bullet. She mocked his muffled cry as she bathed the bullet-mocking that melody's broken hiccup, honking sobs. She loved him. She'd show it.

A white portrait of suits and dresses dried behind the church as family and friends filed onto the lawn.

Everyone stared at the minister, and the groom beside him. On the opposite side of the minister was the row of bridesmaids in their lellow dresses, also waiting for Lennena Bloo as sunlight beggingly asked for its color back from the silk around them. Birches' snowy and coal-splotched bark fought off the sun with that musk of dirty splinters. But the grass refused to let the birches' scent ascend too high up, for something stopped the scents from flying. It was a clean and pleasant musk of May amongst the wedding crowd outside, behind the church. And it made them smile beautifully while watching the groom avoid their glances.

"Nervous?" The minister asked in an excited whisper. Sobek shook his head and cracked a smile. He chuckled. "No, sir."

"Excited?"

Sobek nodded. McKee, next to him, beside the row of groomsmen in grey, kept a caring eye on Sobek as the minister teased. "You'll feel nervous when she walks out."

Pachelbel began to haunt the town of Salem. An elderly quartet made of whining violins and cellos began to weep as ivory roses tried to sound beautiful. The groom awaited that reviving sight of Lennena Bloo. Pachelbel adored to haunt the town of Salem, and family and friends began to haunt the groom with wondering glances.

He looked away. Wondering where his ghost escaped to. His hallucination; still somewhere.

A frantic sprint, she climbed the steps of the church's narrow tower. Impulsive, free and out of breath, she raced through dust above the stairs. The spiralled stone, its curving slope, absorbed her stomping heels with haunting shrieks. The rusting railing kissed her hand with wet regret escaping every sob. Regret escaping every sob. Her clenching teeth, their hiding screams, missing hard the way he loved her every flaw. She raced the wedding's melody with wet regret escaping every sob. Regret escaping every sob.

With flailing arms, her scrambled stop arrived below the wedding bells. Infinitary rooftops watched her face behind rainbow-windows. With no invite, at vulture heights, constricted by the dark and scarlet dress, her black-mascara bleeding gaze began to bulge behind stained-glass petals. Bulged behind the stained-glass petals. Her twisting frown, above the gown that she wished was ivory as a snowfall- froze hearing muffled Pachelbel. Her eyeballs bulged behind stained-glass petals. Lost behind the stained-glass petals.

As she watched through the windows of the church's bell tower, she began to catch the rose-tinted glimpse of the arriving bride, striding towards the groom.

All Vannollia could do was watch, and feel her legs tremble.

Her wedding gift, its chamber's mints that refreshed a loveless future, unexpectedly mocked the ring never wrapped around her finger. Against her side, the sleeping gun, digging deep below her ribcage warning, pulling and pushing to her squeals- her side against the sidearm's jetblack beak. With that revolver's jetblack beak. Her twisted frown, escaping down. It taught her how to forever hold her peace as tears resumed to soak the gown-concealing that revolver's jetblack beak. With that revolver's jetblack beak.

The muffled gasp allowed a pause to Vannollia's crying. Hope. It all left her when the *awww* followed it. She glued her eyes to the sharp and rustic melodies of the stained-glass windows, and watched Lennena Bloo near Sobek, closer and closer.

And, just a second before Lennena Bloo came to a polite stop in front of her groom, all of the shadows in Salem were sucked away. They had vanished, and were eaten by something in the church's bell tower. No one noticed.

The music continued, unconditionally traditional.

"Sobek," Lennena whispered, "your eyes are dry and scarlet. Have you been crying all morning?"

They joined hands without another celestial order.

Sobek paused. He took a deep and heavy breath before allowing himself to lie. "Because of you."

Vannollia pressed her palms against the window, peering down through glossy eyes as Sobek lifted Lennena's veil with slothy fingers. And as Sobek tried absorbing that moment, Vannollia's volcanic soliloquy erupted in the church's bell tower.

She whimpered. "Please don't do it. Don't kiss the other woman. I came back to you."

She knew he looked nervous. He must have still felt her presence, haunting him, right down there with his bride.

Through that ethereal tint of rainbow glass, she saw him smile to Lennena Bloo. She watched the bride allow a smile its freedom out from soon-to-be-kissed lips.

Vannollia shook her head, and pressed herself against the glass even more, hissing after every breathless choke. "Let my heart become your star again. Worship it in the cold of outer-space... the way you always loved me back then."

She watched Lennena Bloo and Sobek keep each other's hands held by the celestial order of the minister, gleefully following his words. Everything felt silent down there as all of Salem stopped to listen to Lennena Bloo and Sobek while ignoring the witch in the bell tower as her unheard vexes casted down against the lawn.

"Let me out of this outer-space." She hissed, wincing. She closed her eyes. The tears yanked down mascara from her squint when she reopened them. She watched the minister's mouth move.

She began to shake her head with frantic dread. The volcano of worry let the sweat escape across her skin, and matt her gown against her flesh. Tears escaped as well, becoming black throughout the race beside the sweat and worried breathing. Her noggin shook a messy pace when Sobek leaned in towards Lennena, holding her face by her chin as he did so.

"No." Vannollia gulped against the glass. She begged with greasy chords escaping every gasp for hope. "No. Nonononono. Please!"

The muffled clapping boomed below the church's bell tower like a hundred baby revolver learning to go off.

Sobek's lips released their lock from Lennena's with that usual gratitude.

"How do you feel?" Lennena asked her husband. Sobek chuckled bashfully, reddened after every member in his family erupted into stupid cheering, as he always knew they would.

"Free." Sobek sighed in that honest confession. "Because of you."

Lennena smiled at her husband as he now appeared to holster some kind of relief. It made his smile genuine than most of the ones he gave to people.

Vannollia muted that eruption that her lungs expelled. Mute. She shrunk. Collapsing down the wall, away from rainbow-petalled windows, that woman began to crumble. Curling in a ball, she raised a silent mouth. It opened, but the pain refused to let a sound escape. She was silent, alone, and bathing in her tears inside the bell tower.

Everyone was happy down below, and she was the rogue anomaly in the church's bell tower.

"I'm such a horrible person." She squeaked so that herself knew this for sure, squeezing out the words. No one reassured her. She thought about how Sobek used to go above and beyond to try, to *try,* and reassure her no matter what it is. Now, she was alone. No one heard her crying, nor would anyone travel up the spiral staircase to see if anyone was crying up there.

She stumbled up, gasping. Through another window in the narrow room of the bell tower, she watched the massive wedding party snake across the street. Couples, children and elders filed into the marble-painted building with cheery smiles that seemed even happier through the stained-glass windows. She sniffled. Every color in the window rejected sympathy for her. The rainbow of glass was too busy smiling at the wedding party.

She pondered. If she was quick enough, she may be able to sneak into the crowd, but her dark-red gown would have made her stick out. She paused, pondered more. She'd hide in the restroom. This thought was finalized by the flutter of her determined blinking.

She took the revolver out, and popped the circular chamber out of the revolver. She let her eyes examine the meaningless serial numbers of the shells which were tucked into the chamber. Six tombs, round and shuttle-like, were sleeping in the black cylinder. Their bases shone almost alike the ring she'd never wear from Sobek. And, in her pause of crying, she wished she had asked him to marry her back in the spring and summertime of 1921 when he loved her.

She pushed the cylinder back into the revolver with a click, and sighed. "I love him."

The restroom in the wedding venue, across the street from the church, was more luminous and less liminal, especially since it was drunk with the molecules that were chattering bridesmaids in lemon-shaded dresses. As the muffled chatter from the ballroom of the venue slithered in through the doorway to perish amongst their gossip, they checked their lashes, hair and earrings before the row of mirrors.

"Where are they?" Polly asked, looking like a different person in the yellow dress that strayed from her usual night-life attire of tassels and flashy threads, loose threads. She puffed her short hair away from her neck, trying to ask the dying gel to try and stay alive for a few more hours. "I never knew weddings took this long."

"They're getting their photos taken in front of the church." Sadie answered. She held a scrap of paper under her chin, reading and rereading between talking and listening to the others in yellow around her. "They should be in the venue shortly."

"I think," Vicky chirped, "he's gonna carry her in."

"He'd probably drop her in the middle of the street, goofy fellow." Esther joked. Sadie was too concentrated in her speech to chuckle with the group. She would have appreciated jumping on that joke though.

"How's the speech?" Polly asked. She looked away from her reflection, turning to watch the concentration turn Sadie pale, and turn her dress more yellow. Some newfound friendliness glimmered in Polly's eyes now, almost as if it was a prisoner who wanted to escape, and live in that glimmer of friendship. The night-life kept it behind bars; loose bars.

"Probably a lot more well written than McKee's." Sadie moped. Vicky chirped. "The wide-eyed groomsmen?"

"He's oddly adorable." Esther noted. "He looked proud, standing next to Sobek."

"Well," Polly chuckled almost sympathetically, "I'm sure he's got a good speech."

Sadie agreed without interest. "He is the best man for a reason, right?"

"Met him before, Sadie?" Vicky asked. Sadie shook her head. "No. I haven't."

"What has Sobek said about him?" Vicky prodded further. Sadie shook her head again.

Polly clucked. "So, good men don't talk about other good men?"

"True." Sadie sighed. "And Lennena never told me about you all until she picked the bridesmaids."

A silence fettered the restroom as Esther, Polly and Vicky remembered how early on she had told them about Sadie. Polly and Vicky almost shared an embarrassed look, but after the conversation from the night before, she felt a little bit welcomed into the family. It was only Vicky and Esther who felt truly embarrassed by this.

"Well, let's go get our seats at the head table, huh?" Sadie spoke as if it was a suggestion by an exhausted soldier. *Let's raid that hill.*

After some more looks in the mirror, the four bridesmaids exited the restroom, giving Vannollia a chance to exit the stall she was hiding in. She strolled towards the row of mirrors, almost ashamed about her scarlet dress as everyone else wore the solar shade of Lennena's blonde hair.

Their lemon colors seemed to linger in the restroom, swirling 'round her, laughing at her crimson dress. While looking in one of the many mirrors above the faucets, she could not erase the image of their smooth and banana-peel-like dresses out of her mind. It almost made her frown, but she was too busy thinking to frown while studying a beauty that never belonged to any holy and yellow colors.

Sne sniffled, swallowed a bit of dread and tried wiping the tears that had seeped into the pores along her pale face below her silver tiara. It held her hair back into a flapper-style bun, almost too short to be a bun as the stalls did not notice that little bulb of tied up hair behind the tiara. Her black, fibbing brunette hair, blended together to form a secretive hair-style- topped with the gleam of her pearl studded tiara like silver coins flipped onto a coal pile of lies.

She managed to get rid of most of the skid marks the mascara left below her eyes, but having been the one to live through that moment inside the bell tower, she felt her face remain a damp and teary mask. With a sigh, she wondered if she should reapply mascara again. No. She knew she may cry again.

"Hello!" Cee chirped upon entering the restroom in a yellow dress of her own.

"Hi." Vannollia replied with that timid explanation of insecurities in her eyes. Spoken so softly, her lips didn't even pop while greeting the older woman.

"Beautiful ceremony." Cee began washing her hands as she talked. "I take it you're from her side of the family."

"Very distant cousin from New York." Vannollia lied, forcing a smile. She turned it all into a sigh. "Everyday's a day there."

Cee retorted, merrily cynical. "Now, everyone knows someone from there, right?"

Vannollia bowed her head. Regret was red around her. Becoming darker, such a dress constricted that elegantly shaped body.

"Is everything alright?" Cee asked, to which Vannollia responded. "Yeah, just-" she lifted her head again, and looked at the old woman as she answered, "-this is my first wedding. Didn't expect it to be that beautiful."

Cee chirped with excitement, digging a flimsy party of fingers through the air. "It was absolutely lovely, wasn't it?"

Vannollia nodded, chuckling and looking away again with a bowing head. "Yeah. Miss Bloo is a lucky lady."

She looked back to Cee, and almost smiled. "He's handsome."

"My grandson is wicked handsome. He's a beautiful person."

"You know," Vannollia forced herself to speak, "he really deserves a kind woman like her."

"Oh," Cee gasped, "their romance is a miracle! She's told you the story?"

Vannollia did not want to hear it, so she lied with a smile again. "I've heard it, ma'am."

"You're awfully pretty. I'm sure Lennena will be a bridesmaid at a wedding of your own soon." Cee said with a candle of hope becoming woken in her. She picked up on *something* about the young woman beside her, and she did not want anyone to be sad. She continued, now puffing up her bushel of hair atop her head. "We all deserve love. All deserve happiness." She then threw in a joke. "Even people from New York."

Vannollia forced a chortle. Her timidness sold the genuineness behind it.

"So, Sobek's your grandson?" Vannollia chirped with the first genuine smile she showed to Cee.

"He is."

Vannollia tried murdering her smile. She remembered how Sobek always wanted her to meet his grandma.

"He must mention you a lot to people."

"I'd hope so." Cee laughed at the thought, very oblivious as to how Sobek would always spit out *you'd love her, Vannollia... she'd love you.*

"So, the bridesmaids wear yellow, but-"

"Lennena insisted I wear yellow too." Cee explained, gesturing to the lemon colored straps of her dress with those theatrical fingers of hers. "Yellow is their color, she says. He calls her his sun, and Lennena and Sadie thought it'd be lovely to have yellow be a theme of the wedding."

"He calls her his sun?"

Cee nodded, unaware of the despair leaking down the pale woman beside her. That grimace would have cracked the mirrors if she ever looked away from his grandma. Cee was too busy looking for recollection in the sink to notice the look upon Vannollia's face.

Cee went on. "He's her planet. She's his sun. They orbit around each other. In that frore, freezing, outer-space, they're in orbit together- safe. Now, bless his heart, I'm sure he calls her his sun because she brightens up his days, but they do orbit around each other. Stop me if I already told you, but Sobek is no scientist, and I don't think he realizes the trueness in him calling Lennena his sun. It's extremely fitting."

Vannollia wished she was deaf. It even just hurt to watch the old woman's mouth move to speak about her grandson loving someone... someone who was not Vannollia. Her, her, her. It had to be her.

"And," Cee began to finish, "I see how faithfully he orbits around her. He was lost for a bit, but-"

"He was lost?"

"Oh. He just had a bloody rotten gal leading him on." Cee crooned. "He's got some other stuff, but- he deals with most on his own, like most men, you know."

"A sun rescued the stray planet." Vannollia sighed.

"There's life upon the surface of his eyes now, twinkling." Cee spoke to alert the mirrors about the newlyweds across the street. "He worships his sun the way the early humans did, worshipping that anomaly- that orbit together."

"Do you think-" Vannollia stammered, "-you reckon that maybe a planet can orbit a black hole?"

There was a pause then that made it feel as if language had never been invented.

"I don't speak for everyone," Cee exclaimed, "but I certainly would not enjoy being anywhere near one of those mindless bulbs of hunger."

"Me neither." Vannollia sighed. She resurrected her voice with defeat still lingering around her fruity voice like the withering gown of night. "But have you seen some of the artist renditions of them?"

Cee exclaimed with excitement. "No."

"They're pretty."

"Looks can be deceiving. No matter what a black hole wears, it's still a black hole." Cee chirped.

Silence arrived to tear apart the orange gown of hope so that the rest of Vannollia's words would sound like the indigo corpse of night; cold, unripe, stale and dishonest fruit.

"But all black holes once were stars, right?" Cee said.

"Is this it then? Only suns deserve Love."

"Look at how a black hole treats everything in its path. It's possible to love anyone, love anything, but does a voracious black hole have it in itself to love?" Cee rambled.

Vannollia glared against her own reflection. "No. There's nothing in it, even as it goes along eating everything in the universe."

"Oh!" Cee said with surprise. "You've been in one?"

Before Vannollia could answer, clapping erupted from the ballroom outside the restroom.

"Oh! Is it them?" Cee cooed before shuffling out of the restroom.

Alone again, Vannollia hushed the final beat of that conversation. "I am one."

Alone again and safe to cry alone again, she watched herself become a wincing woman. That reflection mocked her, copying how she pressed her palm against her chest to feel her heart. *Thumping,* saying not a lick of beautiful reassurance.

She almost heard the star of her heart combust, and collapse from inside out. It sent a shockwave through her ribs, and the aftermath began the first hiccup of sobbing.

Her second hand clasped her mouth as her eyes scrunched back into worried planets- finally realizing there was a black hole beneath them in the heart of their galaxy. The tears ran rougher this time, and the few wrinkles in her fingers got to taste the salt, the wet, regretful, salt. And those two planets of her eyes began melting down towards the black hole that was her heart.

Was it always a beast? A voracious, mindless, beast that only took and used the universe for its own good? She thought so as the pain of her crying reflection shot through her.

In the moment of seeing the woman in the mirror, she almost heard the galactic disaster inside herself; roaring, happy she knew herself now.

With desperate hush, the mirror blushed, afraid to keep her reflection. Unromantically asteroids touched, shamed of sonic revelations. With silver pearls, tiaras dulled, like a ring around the lifeless Saturn. Universally frozen dead- every chance of happiness drowned away. And all her wishes drowned away. Her vineyard curse, the purple blurb of regretful auras that arrive too late, became a mash of cursed liquor as her every chance of happiness drowned away. And all her wishes drowned away.

The star collapsed to sithic black, with that alarming hungry roar. Extinctionary candle wax- the orange dust the void devoured. With sandy rings, the sprinkling of light becoming swallowed down the void, echoed throughout her outer-space as she heeded her black hole heart's abyss. She heard her black hole heart's abyss. He loved it once. She hated love, pushing love away before the explosion. Combusting star, confusing heart, the one he loved without any condition. He loved without any condition.

As the pretty looks of her reflection said nothing, the hungry roar of her black hole heart said everything.

She squinted deeper at her reflection. She remembered the pain resurrecting in his eyes when she appeared in the restroom over an hour ago. How haunted that man appeared, shrivelling into a 19 year old boy again. The pain splotched his pupils like the sut he once married in the coal mines for her.

The muffled party from inside the venue swallowed every gulp of tears she took.

That look in his eyes- like a stranded sailor seeing that anomaly of the black hole appearing in the indigo sky above timid waves. And her eyes were so hopeful as she watched how she terrified him. That horrible contrast ruined her. How he looked at her three years ago- how he looked at her on his wedding day.

She wanted to forget those eyes. She hated that hoarse scream... *BECAUSE OF YOU!* But it was there, constantly falling down the jetblack tunnel of her heart. It was so evident in how he crumbled into the sink, shouted and how he cried- he had been haunted by her for so long. She was his black hole, constantly sucking life out of him, even after she did some strange mercy by breaking up with him.

Was he truly happy? She wondered if he was truly happy if she so easily made him cry in the restroom on his own wedding day. He should've kept it together and talked with her, thanked her for coming. He shouldn't have cried. Did he even know how hysterical he sounded?

Vannollia sniffled, feeling beautiful again before the mirror. She sniffled again, wiped away her tears and nodded.

He was rude. He didn't even offer her an introduction to this holier-than-thou Lennena Bloo.

She shook her head. He was wrong for crying, for getting mad at her. She was trying to make things right, and all he did was mess up.

She remembered the look of pain in his eyes in the church restroom. The cosmic blast *because of you* muffled everything about the universe of emptiness in the venue's restroom. Three years had passed like a lightyear, and the sonic boom of revelation finally reached wherever in the world Vannollia was.

The doorway leading into the wedding venue's ballroom-appearing lobby was obtuse. It was just obtuse enough to allow a good amount of the crowd from inside to foam out with erupting cheers as they all waved on Lennena and Sobek. Their flapping and flailing waving gestured for the husband and wife to cross the street, but the husband and wife were busy talking by the front steps of the church. Their conversation- unheard by the wedding party flooding out of the wedding venue's doorway due to the rushing and roaring of the occasional automobile, and its trollying motorcoaches.

No. The two bundles of families remained clueless aboard the sidewalk, watching, wondering what kept the newlyweds from crossing the street. Even the photographer had hauled her camera across the street and into the grandiose venue already.

"One more. One more." Sobek begged with joy exploding out his chest while holding Lennena's bare shoulders. The white garden of silk, lace, fabric and soft materials shivered below his touch, making her wedding dress become a bashful thing to wear. Her shoulders were alive more than ever in their beige color when piquing out of the ivory dress.

She shook her head, smiling, before leaning forward with shut eyes and puckered lips. Sobek waited at the very last second to close his eyes because he wanted to savor the embarrassed look of happiness on her face when leaning in for another kiss. He closed his eyes. They kissed again. A quick peck. He hated feeling it end.

They opened their eyes. Peace seemed to settle until Sobek cheered again. "Hmmm. One more!"

Lennena craned her neck up. Her giggle died behind her embarrassment. "Sobek!"

"Just one more."

"Fine." Lennena said before closing her eyes and leaning forward again.

They kissed. The wedding party cheered across the street.

It only felt appropriate to draw her into a hug as his palms had been glued to her shoulders for almost two minutes. It was a thankful hug.

Lennena should've heard it coming as they pulled away and out of the hug.

"One more?"

"Sobek!" Lennena groaned with a forgiving smile. "We have to go. They're waiting for us, and-and they're watching. Everyone's seeing you act like a puppy-"

"I don't care who's waiting, who's watching. I'll kiss you in front of everyone in Salem."

Lennena watched the excitement flare, twinkle even, in her husband's eyes.

He began again as they swung their hands together with interlacing fingers. "Look at this moment. I want to kiss forever. Here before the church!"

Lennena smiled.

"We just got married." Sobek cheered in a fresh bark.

"You're acting like a puppy."

"It's like we grew up!" He jabbered. Lennena shook her head, giggling. "Sobek, our families are waiting to congratulate us. We gotta cross-"

"Just one more kiss." Sobek begged as if he knew she'd say yes. He sounded calmer, but the twinkle blasted in his gaze, and Lennena couldn't say no to that.

"I promise-" Sobek mumbled in defeat, "-this will be the final one."

They kissed. Another cheer erupted in the town of Salem.

"Just one more-"

Lennena grabbed his hands with a firmer grip and yanked him and herself across the street in a break in the action of passing automobiles. They crossed the pavement towards the cheers, towards the clapping, towards the laughter.

The rowdy guests, from prison-ship, jumped and cheered amongst the sober. Reactionary laughter slipped out from all below chandeliers. Solar petals, silk of yellow, ruffled 'round the bridesmaids like table cloth. A taunting gust amongst the smiles, oblivious about her wedding gift- unaware of her wedding gift. Family friends, well-groomed and dressed; the wedding party waiting to see them kiss. Jubilant-jumping wedding guests- oblivious about her wedding gift- unaware of her wedding gift.

Sobek had one arm around his wife when McKee began to jig in the center of the crowd. The wedding guests dispersed so there was a circle of space around the dancing man. Laughing, Sobek raised his free arm in approval as he cheered his buddy on. "McKee!"

"How much has he had to drink?" Lennena gasped to her husband. He held her closer while the confused crowd began to clap for McKee.

Sobek smiled at old memories as he answered. "Nothing. That's just him, my love. Look at him go!"

"Come on! Come on!" Sadie broke out of the bundle of cheering guests. She beckoned the husband and wife. "Most of us-" she aimed a judging glance at the jiggling man that was McKee, "-are seated at the bride and groom's table already. Ready for the speeches and meal."

"Sobek wouldn't stop asking for another kiss." Lennena said, unable to stop herself from giggling to the maid of honor.

There was a stage, two or three feet from the ground, at the end of the ballroom-style venue. The collection of bridesmaids and groomsmen (with the exception of McKee) were seated with their yellow dress and ties and folded handkerchiefs blasting out against the birch-white walls of the massive interior. It was such a regal appearing room that it could have taught the eager wedding guests fancy terms in Russian, making their words thick and violently meaningful for the rest of the day inside the ballroom.

The lellow, golden and beige, hues of the ballroom were familiar. It may have been the foreign shade that hatched from the dew upon the field from yesterday. Perhaps it was. It was calming.

Waiters and waitresses scrambled while everyone sat at round tables where full flutes of champagne had already been busy waiting. Bubbles still threatened mute threats near the rims of those thin goblets of glass. The white walls brought out the golden shade about the champagne. Everyone began taking shy sips as the creamy walls fell asleep, content as the room became full with people, making that building feel to be anywhere but in Salem. The town tanned, growing more vintage and dusty by the minute like a Bible collecting dust, but some religion of coins and yellow voices pretended that nothing old awaited anyone outside the massive venue.

"How do you feel?" Sobek asked his wife as he and her sat at the long and rectangular table on the stage with the groomsmen and bridesmaids.

"I'm feeling married." Lennena smiled. It drew the boyish twinkle out of Sobek's eyes, fell into her smile, and sculpted something new between the two of them; intangible.

"How do you feel, husband?"

"Ohhh, lucky." Sobek grunted, scooting his chair closer to the table. "Wicked, wicked, wicked lucky."

"Let our luck last forever then." Lennena chirped with her own glimmer of *just one more* glossing her eyes. *Just one more* became an immortal secret above the white table cloth upon the table as their colliding smiles competed with the glint of their not-yet disturbed champagne.

A symphony of silverware clanging against the champagne flutes began, and was quieted by Lennena and Sobek kissing once more while the waitresses and waiters almost finished placing plates of prime rib on the tables.

Sobek's noggin did a double-take. He looked away from Lennena after the kiss to see the cleanness of the table cloth. But his heart commanded him to look back at her. He did.

As the spotlight of attention made her rub her lips together to bury the dirt of nervousness over her face, Lennena twisted her head around to see her husband's astonished gaze.

"What?" She asked with an embarrassed smile while a faint mumble of almost a hundred conversations layered the floor below the stage.

"N-nothing." Sobek shook his head with the same boyish and puppy-like excitement he had wielded almost a year ago when they began seeing each other. He could have turned red as his best friend aimed her eyes at her husband.

She looked at him the same way she looked at hieroglyphics in the museum; feeling like she knew it, but also wanting to know everything. Above a smile and below the blonde hair that wanted to escape from her white bonnet, the pages in her eyes made all the yellow dresses seem grey.

"What?" She asked. Sobek smiled a greedily beautiful smile the way you do when winning something. "I-I just read something in your eyes."

"Yeah?" She stopped herself from giggling as their plates of food were plopped below their faces. "What did you read?"

He let his eyes answer. *Just one more.* She knew, and smiled before the wedding party at the table on the stage began eating.

As the wedding guests mumbled with mouthfuls, discussing mysteries, the head table on the stage became silent to sort of take it all in. The best astonishment was calm, and the majority of bridesmaids and groomsmen looked as content as newborn babies while the newly weds looked confident in the calmness of having united in holy matrimony. No one had ever chewed so peacefully, so leisurely.

"Do you think this is what it feels like to be the king and queen?" Lennena asked after a few minutes of silence passed for them to eat. Sobek shrugged. "I'm not itching to be a king."

"Why not?" Lennena asked. Sincere in the odd feeling of silence inside the mumble of over a hundred conversations, Sobek was honest. "I feel alright with you. I don't need a court of subjects, you know?"

"You're being too much, Sobek. I'm still reeling from being given the beauty of your broken heart." She had said this as if she was a queen. A pompous accent flared behind her tone in a teasing manner.

Sobek chuckled, almost having forgotten how they slow danced in front of their little red box last night. As she watched her husband shake his head, she also saw the little nervous smile creep across his lips.

"You know," Lennena began with a tilt to her head like a water tower that had just had a limb amputated, "before the girls came to pick me up for the church today, I opened it, and just held it all in my hands... pink sand... it's dusty."

Sobek looked at her.

She moped with longing eyes, remembering something. "Pale and jagged."

He said nothing back to her.

"Why is it dusty, Sobek?"

He thought for a while before moping. "Every little piece matters. It all once used to be part of just one thing."

"I really like that one big piece in there-"

"Yeah?"

"I'm happy it survived the fire." Lennena said with a genuine chortle. "Such a beautiful chunk of... chunk of..."

Sobek smiled a toothless smirk at her, watching his wife stumble to find the words.

"It's like its own thing, and I'm glad it's mine now." Lennena said, then laughed at how goofily the words replayed in her mind. "Don't throw out."

Sobek shook his head. "Hey, we won't, won't we?"

They shared the same *just one more* glance, forgetting some food remained on their plates, and plenty of champagne remained in their flutes. No. They wanted to live it sober. That astonishment of calmness was the ultimate drug of the evening, elevating the smell of their colognes and perfumes that twisted in a waltz with the naturalness they came to love during autumn, winter and spring nights.

The day became a timid evening, welcoming a sunset which no one in the ballroom got to see. White curtains draped every window, and the chandeliers and candles had already given birth to a seemingly eternal sunset in the venue like dim light in a dying light bulb. Everyone had eaten in this medieval light as the threat of something fancy bled from the walls. Sobek and Lennena left the groomsmen and bridesmaids to make their rounds around the ballroom, conversing with the guests.

Vannollia watched the wedding crowd erupt below the chandeliers, below the marble ceilings that could have become the petals of the sky during sunset. It was smooth, the transition that the crowd took from their tables to the floor. They gathered in twos in the spacious middle where tables didn't dwell.

She watched them switch between the slow dancing sway to swinging jigs. The band, which seemed to play from nowhere, was accommodating. Cellos kept the same mellow pace, but the trumpets bleared during fast tunes, but whined a sorry want for attention during slower tunes.

As candles wept, her scarlet dress lingered in a pond of shadows like Aphrodite out of breath, sad to be amongst the mortals. The lemon glare, the solar flare was a dandelion's petals flailing as bridesmaids danced with the groomsmen. She watched them like a vulture watching swans. The skulking vulture watched the swans. The wedding gift, black and snub-nose, its beak remained inside her red-feathered gown. With that revolver in her clothes, she watched them like a vulture watching swans. The skulking vulture watched the swans.

Annoyed, she walked away behind the row of marble pillars. She wandered down the lane between the windows and pillars without a shadow to follow her, for it was a dark perimeter of the ballroom with all the dim light being all alive amongst the dancing crowd inside the middle.

And, that is what she did- pace the perimeter of the ballroom, in the shadows, watching, waiting without any expression dripping down her face.

Amongst the jazzy apology of a mediocre-paced song, Lennena and her husband wandered back over to where Cee was sitting. No one else sat at the table as they were either dancing or had gone home, or went out for a smoke.

"You don't fancy dancing, Cee?" Lennena chirped. She had hushed this casually, the way she'd say it to a friend.

"No."

Sobek could only smile to hear his grandma speak to his wife. The smile was a candle in its own celestial way, like a subject in a museum had come to life. The fabled smile- alive. Happiness like his was such a fairytale. And, for Lennena Bloo, it felt beautiful to own that fairytale.

Cee laughed. "But yah fella earlier. He was a real catch, huh?"

Sobek and Lennena smiled, knowing she was referring to McKee.

Sobek shrugged, keeping that pleasantness on his face. "I don't know where he went off to. Lost in the crowd probably. Did you get the chance to meet him, Grandma?"

She shook her head.

"He's an outstanding man, Grandma." Sobek promised, which truly was a promise as he never said this about anyone.

"Ah!" Cee said, raising an excited finger to keep the married couple's bliss alive. "The bride and groom dance is coming up."

"All eyes on us." Lennena said. At this, Sobek put his arm around her waist with her forearm whispering the gentle *just one more* against her lower back. She felt less nervous because of this, and he kept his arm around her.

"So," Cee nodded, "I heard you two've had some practice."

"Wh-what?" Sobek stuttered with his nervous smile.

"Oh, Lennena!" Cee cheered, remembering something.

Sobek smiled to hear how beautiful his wife's name sounded when his grandma said it.

Cee went on. "I met your cousin from New York. I never caught her name though."

It was concerning to watch confusion drape Lennena's face, especially when she refused to let the smile go. Her eyes disagreed with how she smiled, but she wanted to keep it all in that moment.

Lennena broke the news the way a mother tells her son about his puppy dying. "But Cee, I don't have any family from New York."

Sobek's smile faded until it was a smile without happiness. It was still there, but it was there in the way a body lies in a coffin. His eyes even frowned at his grandma.

There was a pause that made them feel like fools in a carnival as the band continued letting a jazzy parade of riffs loose around the wedding guests.

"What did she look like?" Lennena asked. Cee took no time to remember the woman as she answered. "She strayed from the pack, right? Not one bit of yellow bout her. She was wearing this wicked elegant tiara-"

Sobek rubbed his lips together. He grasped his wife tighter, keeping her close to him with his arm around her waist.

"-and she was in this absolutely bloody-red gown." Cee continued. "It was similar to what the flappers wear, but this was a promiscuous gown in a subtle way, not subtle enough for me to think this though."

"Weird." Lennena chirped. She let her smile become a careless life again upon her lips.

Cee shrugged. "This was hours ago, and I haven't seen her since, so, c'est la vie. I just thought it was peculiar."

The two ladies were too busy nodding in agreement to notice the tired look in Sobek's eyes. It was only evident in the canvas of those eyes; he had not slept for three years in that moment.

"A red dress." Lennena hummed. She looked around, only seeing grey suits, black suits, yellow dresses and some rebellious lime dresses in the crowd of dancing wedding guests. She brought her attention back to Cee. "I don't see any red in the crowd. Do you, Sobek?"

Sobek checked- pretended to check at least. "N-no. All I see is lellow."

It slipped out. He quickly shot his voice into the candle-steam-scented air again. "Y-yellow."

"You're not scared of women in red dresses, are you, dear?" Lennena asked her husband with a smile telling him everything was alright.

"No." He uttered, stone-cold. "Just itching for the dance, eh. Our slow dance with *everyone* watching us."

Lennena whined the way she would if she saw a puppy. "Baby."

Her eyes beaconed the *just one more* to him, so he kissed her with a quick peck.

The tune stopped before one of the band members finally revealed where the band was playing from; a balcony over the entrance of the ballroom. He cheered in an accent that seemed to come from some Louisianan paradise a hundred years ago.

"Ladies and gentlemen!" He cheered. "I would ask this dance to disperse, to make way for the newly wedded husband and wife to dance!"

The bundle of yellow in the middle of the ballroom heeded. Everyone melted back away to their tables. Some were holding hands, coupled up now. In the absence of everyone upon the dance floor now, not a single breath of anything scarlet could be seen.

Cee smiled, clapping her hands together as she hummed in a tone that belonged to say *congratulations.* "Good luck, you two. Have fun."

"We will." Lennena ribbitted with the excitement leaking from all around her in a yellow hue of beautiful freedom. She took a light move out of Sobek's hold, then took his hand. She began leading him away towards the ominous space in the middle of the ballroom like Death pulling a coward out of the trench.

"I love you, Grandma." Sobek jabbered in a half cheer. She giggled back. "I love you too. I love the both of you."

"We love you too, Cee." Lennena said in a full cheer just as the music began in a soft apology, softer, slower than ever.

Cee watched them step into their positions- standing, looking at each other, beginning to sway, holding one another. She smiled.

"Good." Sadie said, returning to sit with her grandma. "Just in time to see if he's really good at this."

"Oh. He's fine." Cee said, paused, then whispered to her granddaughter. "You wanna know something wicked odd, Sadie?"

"Yeah, Grandma?" Sadie said while her eyes remained an intent spectator with a ticket to the two-soul show.

"I was talking to Lennena and Sobek just now-"

Sadie crooned in an exhausted yawn. "Yeah? The mister and misses."

"-because I met some woman in the restroom. She was this young, pretty, woman who said she was a cousin of Lennena's cousin from New York."

Sadie froze.

"But I told Lennena," Cee explained with a nonchalant shrug of her hands, "and she said she doesn't have any family from New York."

"You said New York?"

"This woman said New York."

Sadie struggled keeping her jaw closed. She got up, hissing in a whisper. "Grandma, I'll be right back."

"Alright, sweetheart."

Sadie fled to the restroom.

Cee propelled from her seat to follow her granddaughter. They met in the restroom with her own entrance interrupting Sadie's bombardment of checking every stall in the restroom.

"What's the matter?" Cee asked.

Alarm erupted down Sadie's face as she stood next to the very last stall in the restroom with its door open. All the doors were open. Defeat fettered her parted lips as she exhaled. "Grandma, I-I think that was Vannollia you spoke to."

"There's no way." Cee disagreed with confidence. "Darling, the p-"

"Grandma," Sadie protested with an unsteady voice as she took a lanky stroll past the row of open stall doors, "it-it is possible. It's possible. She called a week ago, asking about him."

"No way."

Sadie nodded. The grandmother and granddaughter shared a sobering look of concern. Sadie's eyes tried curing the disbelief in Cee's until their expressions molded into the same mask of disbelief, concern and wonder.

Slightly hiding their expressions on account of wanting to keep the wedding celebration in order, they swept themselves out of the restroom, and split up in the venue, searching for the woman in the scarlet gown with the silver tiara.

A question lingered in Cee's eyes while she was looking. *Why would she call for him?* Sadie's eyes had a vacancy of expression. Her eyes were glazed with silent determination as she caught faint glimpses of the newly wedded husband and wife in the lonely firepit of the ballroom floor. The scene came in and out, in and out, in and out as she raced past tables of people, pillars and folks standing to watch the little slow dance.

Sobek and Lennena took hold of one another amongst the whining of melancholic pianos and violins as the thunder of cellos boomed, rolling with regret, with the sweetest sorrow.

The whiskey shade the candles gave bled amongst the champagne's yellow. Luminously the ceiling blazed for the newly wedded couple.

With lellow pelts, the asteroid belts of wedding guests' exhausted eyes, atmospherically emptied out while wondering about the time. With Spartan yawns, they slouched and slumped, watching solar secrets burn the cosmos. A peaceful boredom sprawled away with no blackness eclipsing that orbit. Nothing eclipsing that orbit. A calm exhaust, propelling off and flailing slow away from the sun's surface, began to haunt the ballroom's lott with no blackness eclipsing that orbit. Nothing eclipsing that orbit.

Something twinkled in her husband's eyes as he desperately tried to appear okay.

"Lennena." He choked. He gulped as he held her hips while they swayed in the slow orbit upon the floor, alone. The planetary noggins of seated wedding guests remained in their own dormant galaxies, watching the lonely solar system in the middle of the ballroom. Like the silent and curious fizz of the universe, their starry eyes watched the dance to the tune of a sorrily sweet melody from above them.

"Yes?" Lennena croaked, unafraid.

Sobek scanned his wife's eyes to see if she was alright as he stammered in a soft whimper. "Lennena, I love you. I really love you."

"What's the matter?" She asked with a sweet chime as soft as a swing squeaking in the merry breath of May.

"I-I know this woman that my Grandma saw." Sobek confessed, holding onto his wife more tightly as their orbit remained the slowest pace. "She approached me in the church restroom right before the wedding, telling me she loved me, and I told her to leave."

A little bit of shock made Lennena wince, but she absorbed the information in a quick way.

"Wh-who?"

"Bu-but she's not a good person, Lennena." Sobek said with rubbing lips. His eyes never strayed from Lennena's as she listened to him, keeping her hold light around his neck. "And she lies. I don't know if she's still here-"

"Who is she?"

"Someone I was in a relationship with three years ago. But I love you, Lennena. If we see her, if she's still here, I don't know what she'll try to say to you- if -if she intrudes in our dance."

Sighing, Lennena shook her head. She kept her gaze a calming one, refusing to let it stray from her husband. She heard the way his voice rattled at some phantom pain, some memory she had no idea about. She had heard *everything* from him, except about any former relationships, so her caring eyes found a reason to believe him. She believed his tone, and how his eyes still wept *just one more,* even as he was nervous.

"Hey. Hey." She slipped her palm onto his cheek, holding it with the command that he not look away. She watched how it sprayed water on the fire behind his eyes. "You called me your angel last night. I am. I am, Sobek, alright? And whoever this stranger is, whatever they say or did, you have me. I'm right here."

She watched him nod. The embarrassment was subtle on his face, but as she held his face, relief showered him.

"And look who has you." Lennena said in a promising hush as couples began to melt back onto the dance floor. "Not her. Not this stranger from your past. I'm right here. I'm right here."

She watched him become calm, feeling how lighter his hands felt on her hips now. She had come to know he liked repetitive things, like poetry, so she reassured him as they orbited in the center of the galaxy of slow-dancing men and women while the beautiful melody wept.

"Baby, I'm right here."

Sobek nodded. He hushed. "I love you, Lennena. I love us. I just don't want anyone to try and disturb today, any of our days-"

"Darling." Lennena shook her head. A few more couples crept onto the floor below the wilting chandeliers as their dim apologies fell like orange petals. "Sobek, no one ever could. I believe you. I trust you. I love you."

Sobek nodded. His eyes said it all. He adored how her palm felt against his face, healing, healing, healing as her skin radiated an angelic way in the sunsets of the chandeliers.

"You are my sunsettress, Lennena."

They kissed. Their lips parted. Their eyes opened again to reveal that *just one more* that became a painting of eternal blankness in the universe around them as they continued slowly swaying in orbit in the center of the galaxy of slow-dancing wedding guests.

Vannollia swept out from the pillars of dancers, rolling to the husband and wife like thunder. That uninvited black hole barged into their solar system with ambient roaring, hungry and lightless as it surrounded itself with the dust of dying light. Light bended for her as her beyond black and hollow presence swallowed every whiskey orange and lemon lellow the way a battlefield collects the dead.

Sobek and Lennena twisted their heads to meet the quiet hatred in the eyes of Vannollia with not-yet shocked glances, the way a roman must have looked into the uncharted sky. Their married eyes just searched for a reason why before their brains computed anything beyond that ambient wonder.

No one even got the chance to open their mouths.

Confusion had not even perished from Lennena's eyes yet when the intruder raised a revolver from her side, extending it towards the husband and wife, extending it towards her husband. Shock tried yanking Lennena's mouth open as her palm tackled her husband's collar, right near his pink tie in some sorry attempt of pushing him away.

The wedded couple's sprouting shared surprise met the jetbleak gleam of the snub-nosed and jetblack beak of Vannollia's wedding gift. Their vision became murky when the flash exploded in a blast of smoke.

Lennena heard nothing after the clap of metallic thunder had exploded in front of them, so the following screams in the ballroom were mute, if not muffled. Deaf. Everything became blackly mute in the thunder of instant grief.

As the smoke settled, and the flash rang in her field of vision like a glare from the sun tattooing itself in her eyes, she felt her husband slink down in her arms. She tried holding him up. That shocked expression was even more terrifying on his face than hers as if he saw something which she didn't.

Sadie broke out of the crowd of dancers, too late. She erupted into a similar shock that kept Lennena Bloo in that cocoon of unravelling trauma.

Lennena tried, she desperately tried, holding her husband up as his weight collapsed against her chest. In her clutching of him, she began to feel the warmness trickle down her forearm. The velvet river left from a spheric tear in his suit. Like a disobedient paint, it refused to stop anywhere on her forearm or wedding gown. It just trickled down her skin as the blood oozed out from the hole in her husband's chest.

A bushel of wedding guests tackled Vannollia. The revolver was yanked away. She fell, slipping onto her back on the marble floor below the big bang of shouting family and friends.

Lennena had no tears as she fell to the same slothing pace as her husband, holding him, holding him as he collapsed. She clutched his chin, running her thumb over his parted lips, feeling his weak breath beg, beg and beg. He squinted up at her, watching her cry his name amongst the nor'easter of violent tears which scalded such a beautiful face.

His paling eyes, began to hide, watching every scream's eruption. Obituaries in her eyes watched the dusty light's exhaling. A plea of how, her gurgled shout, became a muffled gust amongst her squeals. The chandeliers, their farewell blinks, witnessed her hold his head against her chest. Her prayers for Love escaped her breath. The lingered snear, revolvers wear settling around the married two collapsed. Anniversaries disappeared as every hope for Love escaped her breath. Her life with him escaped with Death.

Lennena Bloo cradled Sobek in her arms as her knees dug into the hard, cold, bloody surface of the floor. Many more tears had slipped from her glossy cheeks and married the dampened mess that became his suit. The red splotch had already finished expanding over his chest, and he looked to be asleep now. His head was a flimsy soldier, following every shake of his wife's unstill arms. She was too busy cradling her husband's lifeless body to hear Sadie and Cee asking if he was alright. All they had to do was hear past the deafening thunder of the revolver shot from a minute ago, and hear her screams. All they had to do was aim curious glances of dread over Lennena's shoulders to see the sleeping face of their loved one. A brother. A grandson. A husband.

As her face contorted into a scrunch of hatred, Sadie twisted around and dove into the crowd that was pummelling Vannollia. She broke in through the wall of people with ruthless hands, pushing everyone aside so Vannollia got to see the face of a grieving little sister. Her nails, her fists, her clenching grimace demanded to know why as she lunged upon the woman on the floor in the scarlet dress.

Cee came to a slow revelation with her eyes upon her grandson's face. It looked corrupted as Lennena's fingers tried grabbing something back from the void, slipping her fingertips down her husband's face, begging, pleading, hoarsely whining for a reaction from his body.

She was left alone, cradling her husband's body on the ballroom floor as Sadie and McKee stomped up and down on Vannollia's noggin and chest, crushing out the wine across the ballroom floor amongst the crunch of bone.

Lennena Bloo cried it all. Sniffling, dipping her head against his forehead so their black and blonde hair could meet a final time.

His paling face was unreactive forever. Lennena Bloo cried for just one more life with him forever, forever. The lellow widow, doomed to mourn just one more forever, forever, grasping onto him forever, forever.

So, Lennena Bloo screamed over her dead husband, holding his face as her own face desperately repeated *just one more... don't throw out.*

www.ingramcontent.com/pod-product-compliance
Lightning Source LLC
LaVergne TN
LVHW041110150826
845673LV00007B/2001

* 9 7 9 8 7 5 9 5 8 7 6 5 1 *